OPEN Road

KRIS BUTLER

A TATTOOED HEARTS NOVELLA

Open Road
Tattooed Hearts Novella
Kris Butler

First Edition: August 2022
Published by: Incognito Scribe Productions LLC
Kris Butler

Proofreading: © 2022 by Owlsome Author Services
Formatting: © 2022 Incognito Scribe Productions LLC
Cover Design: © 2022 Incognito Scribe Productions LLC

❀ Created with Vellum

OPEN *Road*

KRIS BUTLER

Contents

Blurb

At one time, I thought my life was planned out. Then a stalker entered my life and tossed my world upside down. After everything settled, I thought I was ready to get back to normal, every day life. But when a mysterious letter arrived, it felt like the answer I'd been waiting for.

My whole life, I'd spent in two places, never straying far from home. It was time for this baby bird to fly. Along with my three boyfriends, we found ourselves on a trip of a lifetime with new experiences to uncover. From conventions, to famous monuments, and all the hotels inbetween, it turned into a trip I wouldn't soon forget.

So when a bully arrived and tried to steal our happiness, I knew it was time to take a stand—even if that meant singing on a stage.

Are you brave enough to discover what the open road has to offer you?

Foreword

This book is intended for readers 18+ due to content and language. There are explicit sexual scenes. This story is a why-choose relationship with LTGBQ+ characters within.

This book deals with a lot of laughter, cute animals, and might make you want to get a tattoo and go on your own open road adventure. You have been warned.

Chapters 1-4 are a recap from the bonus section of part three in the Tattooed Hearts Completed Duet. If you don't need that, feel free to start at chapter 5, The Letter.

To my grandmother—for all the RV adventures you took me on every summer as a kid. Thanks for showing me hidden gems of the world.

Chapter One

THE BEEPING DREW me to its position, and I squatted, bending to look under the bed. The idea of having a robot vacuum had sounded perfect in theory, but the more I used it, the more I loathed it. Mainly because it always seemed to get stuck when it was my turn, and I ended up chasing it more than it cleaned. I'd already be done with vacuuming if I'd done it the old-fashioned way to begin with.

"Screw you, Matilda."

The blinking light on the machine mocked me as I wiggled under the bed, reaching to grab it. Tugging, I hauled it back toward me, panting with the exertion that it took. Once I finally had it free, I sat back on my heels, staring daggers at it.

"What's got your panties in a twist this time, Matilda? Hmm?"

Flipping it over, I saw what the problem was. My hair had raveled around one of the wheels, jamming it. Fiddlesticks! Rolling my eyes, I dragged it with me to the kitchen, so I could get the scissors. I didn't dare touch Simon's again. He'd acted like I'd committed the biggest crime when I'd used his one time. So picky!

I almost had all the hair cut out and unraveled when the front door opened. I didn't turn to see who it was, though, too immersed in my project to stop at this point. I was determined to win against Matilda.

"Not today, Matilda, not today! Ho-rah!" I shouted, raising the hairball into the air in victory and mimed silent people clapping for me and calling my name. Naturally, I bowed, taking the congratulations. "Thank you, thank you."

"Some days, I wonder about you, Peach."

"Just some days?" I smirked but didn't turn, putting the pieces I'd dismantled back in. Arms bracketed me on the counter, his front pressing into my back as his head rested on my shoulder.

"Hmm, good point. What are you doing?"

"Winning my fight against Matilda."

"I still can't believe you named the vacuum." I shrugged, his head moving slightly at the gesture.

"It talks, moves, and causes me annoyance; therefore, it gets a name. Besides, you named your dick." I laughed, and he only growled in my ear more, choosing to ignore that part.

"Your criteria is suspect."

I shrugged again as I finished the last piece and snapped it closed. Flipping it over, I bent down to place it on the floor, momentarily forgetting Slade was behind me. In the process, I brushed my butt up against him. He cursed and an evil smile grew on my face as a thought entered my head. Hitting start on Matilda, I listened to it sing as it started back on its merry way to finish the job.

Slowly, I stood back up, grazing my butt more purposeful this time against him. His hands clamped down on my hips, stopping my motion.

"Oh, sorry."

Slade leaned down, his voice husky as he whispered in my ear. "I don't believe you for one second, Peach, but I'll let you make it up to me if you've followed directions." My breath hitched, a shot of electricity shooting straight to my clit at his words. His hands started to move forward, stopping at the hem of my dress. "But if you've been disobedient, then I'll have to change tactics. So, tell me, Peach, will I be rewarding us both, or only me?"

Biting my lip, I looked over my shoulder, catching his eyes filled with heat as I pressed back into him more. He groaned, but his eyes didn't drop, waiting for my answer.

"Find out."

His pupils dilated, and I felt the cool air hit my legs as he wrenched up my dress, plunging his fingers upward. The sudden intrusion had me gasping, and my eyes rolled back as I felt myself adjust to him.

"Fuck, Peach." Slade started to move his fingers, not wasting any time as he coated himself in my wetness, rubbing my clit with his thumb. I spread my legs wider, wanting to feel more of him, brushing my butt against him again. It was all it took, and he lifted me up on the counter higher, my feet leaving the ground as he spread me apart.

"Seems you can follow directions when properly motivated, Peach." I didn't respond; there was no way I could anyway as he began to lick up my center from behind. His hands spread me open, my thick thighs pressed tight in his hands, and I was a puddle to his whims as I lay on the kitchen island.

"Shit, you're so wet. I fucking need you, Peach."

I whimpered as he pulled away, cool air hitting my exposed parts, too lost in my desire to understand what he'd said entirely. Slade gathered me in his arms, and I squeaked at the change of position, clinging to him.

He stared down at me, and I saw the hunger I'd missed in his words. Slade stopped a few feet later, dropping my feet to the floor before yanking the dress over my head, stopping to stare at my naked body on display for him. "Fuck, you're so perfect."

He greedily eyed my pussy, licking his lips, and I moved to unbuckle his belt, no longer wanting to wait either. Together, we managed to free his cock as it sprang forward. I wrapped my hand around him, but Slade grunted, stepping back, so I was out of reach.

"Hands on the couch, and put that perfect peach ass up in the air."

Turning, I braced myself on the back of the couch, leaning forward, so my butt stuck out. His hands gripped my hips, pulling me back to him as he slid into me in one move. "Fuck," he groaned. "Each time I'm in you, Peach, it feels like the first. Hold on, I'm not going to be gentle."

His fingers bit into my skin as he pulled back and slammed into me, the force moving the couch forward. I moaned at how he filled me, and I was soon lost in ecstasy as we worked together. Sweat pebbled on my skin, and the delicious feeling of his balls slapping my clit had me so close. I just needed a little more.

"Well, it seems I got home at just the right time."

My eyes opened to find Simon standing in front of the couch, a sexy smile on his face. His silver hair was windblown, adding to his sex appeal as he stripped off his shirt and shucked his pants. He prowled forward, kneeling on the cushion and bringing his dick close to my lips.

I grinned at him, lifting a hand to stroke him. "Oh, do you want me to lick it?"

"Lick it, suck it, blow it. I don't care as long as you touch it." He laughed, and I pulled him closer to my lips, taking him into my mouth. His moan joined ours, and I knew I was close now.

Simon leaned forward, pulling Slade to his lips as they kissed over me. When his hand drifted down in between us, I didn't know how it was possible, but that last little touch was what I'd been needing, and I tipped over, my orgasm exploding in me.

My muscles contracted, and I squeezed Simon's dick as I moaned. He spilled down my throat as he came, and I felt Slade tense, holding me tight a few seconds later. Our panting filled the room, along with smells of sex, and I smiled happily as I laid my head against the couch.

"Looks like you saved the best twin to close," Zane teased, pulling my attention to him. Slade grumbled, but didn't say anything as he slowly pulled out of me. I crooked a finger, lazily calling him to me.

"I have a better idea." He walked over and lifted me up, and I sighed happily again. I used to be self-conscious of them doing that, worried I weighed too much. Either they decided to prove me wrong by always picking me up now, or I'd been worried about nothing, I didn't know, but the fact was, they did, and I loved it each time.

Zane walked around the couch and sat down on it, with me in his lap. Brushing my hair back, he cupped my cheeks, holding them. "How was your day, Noxy girl?"

"Better now. Matilda was a honky-tonk, though." Zane smiled, not annoyed with my weird naming of inanimate objects.

"Hmm, well, I'll try to make it better then." He kissed my neck, bringing goosebumps to my skin, and I felt myself growing ready to go again. Pushing up his shirt, I pulled it over his head, tossing it to the floor. My hands rubbed against his bare chest as he peppered kisses down my neck, his hands exploring my naked skin.

Grunting to my left had me turning my head as he sucked on the dip of my neck. It was a battle to keep my eyes open to watch S&S together as he did that.

Slade had Simon pressed against the side of the couch now, his head pulled back as he kissed him, his hand stroking his cock, bringing it erect again. The show made me rock against Zane, the roughness of his zipper reminding me he was still partially clothed. Lifting up, I unzipped his pants and pushed his boxers down as much as possible to free his length. His dick sprung up, and I got lost in stroking it as I greeted it.

Zane and Simon's moans filled the room, and I wanted to be part of it. Putting myself over him, I lowered myself down until I felt Zane fully sheathed in me. He smirked when I moaned, his hands going to my butt cheeks to lift me. He started to move, lifting me as he plunged up, and I laid on his chest, pleasure coursing through me. Opening my eyes, I watched as Slade lubed himself and then Simon, pressing him further down into the couch.

Reaching a hand, I interlaced my fingers with Si's, feeling the connection of all three of us at that moment as Slade started to fill him. The twins seemed to be competing to see who they could make cum first, or last the longest, as they both began to thrust with abandon in their counterparts.

Within seconds, I saw stars, my clit rubbing against his pelvic bone and sending me over the edge, a loud scream leaving me as I came.

As I regained my breath, Zane didn't stop, pistoning up into me with such strength, I wondered how he was doing it. Simon's hand tightened, followed by a moan and shout. "Fuck, babe, I'm cumming." I watched as he jerked his cock, his cum spraying the couch in the process.

"Me… too…" Slade panted, stilling himself in Simon as he held onto him. Zane heard it and let himself finally go, coming with a roar in me.

"I win." He grinned down at me, and I rolled my eyes, content to lay on his chest for a moment.

"If chores end that way every time, I think I have a new appreciation for them."

The guys chuckled, the sound resonating in my bones. It was one of my favorite sounds.

"Peach, if you do anything pantiless, I can guarantee I'll be balls deep in you before you're done. Just saying." Slade eyes me, heat flaring at the thought. My cheeks flamed as I met his eyes, and I knew he meant it.

"Well," I started, clearing my throat. "I think I, *you know*, um, drip too much for that to make it a thing."

"Nonsense. I want all my cream, Peach."

Well, okay then, who could argue with that?

Chapter Two

THANE

PUSHING OPEN THE DOORS, I shifted the box in my hands that Slade had wanted. He looked up at my entrance, nodding to a place I could put it.

"That the last one?"

"Yeah." Exhaling, I wiped the sweat that had developed on my brow from all my trips. "What do you need me to do?"

Slade looked at me, his face blank. "I'm glad you're here. I just wanted you to know that."

It took me a second to realize he wasn't joking. "I'm glad to be here, too. It's nice spending time with you."

He nodded, returning back to the table tray he was organizing. "Have you talked to Dad lately?"

"Yeah, he likes what you've done so far and wants to schedule a time to visit. He wants you to meet his new girlfriend. I think you'll like her. She's different from the others."

He sighed, but nodded. "Fine. Can you put the last of these supplies in her suite? Then head back to the house. I need to take a shower and a nap. I'll be glad when this is done, so I get some actual sleep. Keeping Lennox away has been hell."

"Sure thing." I smiled, wiping the counter down.

He walked around the desk, squeezing my shoulder on his way out. "It's good to have you here, Brother. You ready for some ink yet?" He smiled at me, a twinkle in his eye.

I laughed, shaking my head. "No. It would have to be special to get me over my fear of needles. Even putting these in the cabinet makes me want to pass out."

"It doesn't even hurt. It's all in your head."

"Says the man with more tattoos than he has skin left for one."

He shrugged. "Trust me. You'd be fine. I'll just make Peach do it. You won't say no to her."

"You wouldn't!" I gasped, clutching my chest as my heart started to race.

Slade grinned evilly before walking out, not dismissing my statement. Quickly, I organized the supplies and finished the hardware of all the drawers and cabinets. I was handier with a hammer than

Slade, so I'd volunteered to finish the last touches before the reveal, wanting to add my own little surprise. It felt nice to be needed too, if I was honest. I was slowly finding my spot in my brother's life again, and among the group. It was a sense of belonging and peace I'd craved for years, finally coming to fruition. And all because a girl named Lennox decided to love us both.

Placing the last candles, I queued up the music, leaving it ready to play for later. I made sure everything was perfect. Grinning, I couldn't wait for her to see it. I knew Lennox would love it.

Chapter Three

SLADE

MY KNEE BOUNCED as I sat next to Simon on the couch, ready to go. We'd only been at Peach's parents' house for thirty minutes, but I was prepared to show Lennox the surprise already. We'd stopped by to distract her and give Thane time to finish up some of the last-minute details I'd needed his help with. It was nice having him here, but I didn't want it to go to his head.

Despite our careful distractions, Lennox had still been giving me the side-eye all day, and I knew she was close to figuring out our secret. I hated keeping things from her, even if it was a surprise. It just didn't feel natural not to tell her every detail of my day now. I never wanted to go back to where lies were our norm.

"Slade, would you like another piece of pie?" Robin asked, pulling my attention back to the room.

"No, ma'am. That was delicious, but I'm stuffed." I patted my stomach, smiling at Lennox's mom. She'd always been nice to me, even when I hadn't been the nicest to her daughter, and for that, I made sure to always show her respect.

"Well, you know where more is if you change your mind, sweetie." She grinned kindly at me before she walked back into the kitchen. Simon elbowed me, leaning over to whisper.

"I think she's trying to fatten you up."

I raised an eyebrow, not getting his meaning. "And?"

"Southern woman's way to a man's heart. Maybe she thinks if you like her pie, you'll want to be part of the family?"

I rolled my eyes, not buying it. It didn't matter. Lennox was it for me, regardless if her mother made a killer apple pie. Her daughter happened to make the best peach, and it was my favorite.

"How much longer?" I whispered, shifting again. Simon checked his phone discreetly, not wanting to grab Lennox's attention as she worked on a puzzle with Noah and her father at the table.

"He's finished. Let's pop over to my parents real

quick, and then he should be here. I have one thing I want to grab."

Nodding, I stood with him and waited for him to tell the others where we were headed. Lennox gave us a look, suspicion heavy in her gaze, and I hated she was feeling left out. I didn't want her to feel that way. She was my whole world, and the sooner she knew that, the less anxious I'd feel.

Walking into Simon's childhood bedroom, a new idea emerged in my head. He went to the bookshelf, grabbed something, and then turned around, catching my face.

"No."

"What?" My lip lifted up slightly, giving away my intention.

"Uh-huh, I see that look. I know that face." Simon grabbed me by the hips, pulling our bodies together, looping his fingers into the belt loops to hold onto me. "If we weren't about to show Lenn the surprise you've been working on all month, then I'd be right there with you. You're just nervous and wanting to distract yourself, but it would be at Peach's expense, and neither of us want that. So, come on. Keep your snakezilla in your pants, and let's go and rock our girl's world—figuratively speaking."

He grinned, pecking my nose and letting go of the loops before he walked out. I knew he was right, but my cock didn't like the idea of waiting as it strained against my zipper. Following him, I took some deep breaths, reminding myself she'd love it. Plus, it wasn't like I hadn't been drawing this tattoo for close to ten years now.

It was time I inked my girl, declaring to her and the world she was mine.

Chapter Four

SIMON

WE SHUFFLED INTO THE STORE, Lennox in front of Slade, as he covered her eyes. Thane went around, turning on the lights, and the shop slowly came into view. The smell of fresh paint and plaster was still thick in the air, and it tickled my nose. The candles Thane had placed should help once they were lit. I had to give it to him, the place looked incredible.

Slade had spent the past week drawing and painting a mural that covered the main wall in front of the desk. It was a modge-podge of images that represented all of us. There were tiny envelopes, stars, hearts, fire, music notes, her yellow bug, a motorcycle, and even a peach. The bigger picture was of the four of us, with Lennox in the middle. It was beautiful how he'd interconnected every little detail of our lives.

Thane had spent most of the day putting little glow-in-the-dark stars all over the place as well, finishing it off with candles and music. I helped him light the last candle, and he hit play on the remote, the speakers coming to life with her voice. I heard her gasp as she recognized it, and she tried to turn her head to find where it was coming from.

"Okay, you can open your eyes now, Peach."

Slade dropped his hands, shoving them into his pants as he stepped back, fear she'd hate it written all over his face. This was step one in his big plan.

"Whoa," she exclaimed. She covered her mouth as she tried to take in all the details. "You did all of this for *me*?"

"Of course, we love you, Lemon," I said, Slade having lost his words.

"I love you, guys, too."

She reached out, grabbing all of our hands, squeezing them as she tried to get her emotions under control. She kept going back to the mural and finally dropped our hands so she could walk over to it to inspect it.

"This is incredible, Slade. I knew you were talented, but this is amazing. I just…" she trailed off as she looked closer. "It's like a 'Where's Waldo?' of our lives."

Slade's shoulders relaxed, and he grabbed her hand, pulling her to the door of the next room.

"This one's yours."

"Mine? Do you mean? But I thought—"

"I just told you no because I wanted it to be a surprise. So, I agreed to let you be out there with the others, but come on, Peach. Do you really think I let just everyone gawk at you? I want to limit it as much as possible," he growled, pulling her to him, his alphahole tendencies returning.

I watched as she melted into him, and I smiled, loving the way they loved one another.

"We did good," Thane said, bumping my shoulder. I nodded, unable to look away.

"Yeah, we did."

Slade kissed her quickly, releasing her to drag her into the studio he'd customized for her. Lenn's eyes grew huge as she walked in, her mouth falling open as she spun around, taking everything in. "This is amazeballs."

Slade stood back, watching her. He hadn't spared any expense on the space, making it a tattoo artist's dream studio.

"Well, get comfortable, Peach. It's time you got some ink. First one is yours."

Squealing, she jumped into the chair, and Slade began his setup. Sitting back on the couch, I relaxed now that the reveal had gone well. I knew it would, but Slade's anxiety had started to rub off on me. Lenn would've been happy with a janitor's closet. She just wanted to be part of it.

I opened my phone and returned to scrolling through jobs online, looking for something that interested me. The salon had reopened this week after the explosion, but I hadn't felt like returning there. I loved doing hair, but lately, I'd been bored, wanting something more. So, I took it as my chance to step into something new. I just hadn't found what it was yet. Thane sat next to me, opening a book Lenn had loaned him.

"Lay back and lift your shirt," Slade ordered Lenn and then started to place the tattoo he'd sketched where he wanted it. He hadn't let anyone see it yet, so I was just as curious as Lenn. She grumbled about being kept in the dark even longer, and glad she'd worn jeans today so he didn't get any ideas about tattooing her butt. Slade ignored her, going about his business, wanting it to be perfect.

Thane and I became absorbed on the couch while Slade worked, not noticing the passage of time. An hour had passed when he spoke up, surprising me. "I never knew people actually had these types of relationships," Thane murmured, turning the page, almost making me jump at the noise.

"Which one are you on?"

"Book 2, Shattered Secrets."

"Ah, have you met Tyler yet?"

"Yes. Though, I kinda wanted to punch that one chick. She has more nicknames than Stalker Thane."

Laughing, I shook my head but didn't disagree, glad that chapter of our life was over. I was scrolling aimlessly at this point, about to give up, when something caught my eye. Going back to it, I read it. Then reread it. Could it work? But the shop…

A semi-plan started to form in my head, but I wasn't sure if everyone would be on board. Clicking on the link, I read all the information. It sounded perfect; I just didn't know if I could convince everyone.

"What's got you biting your lip?" Thane asked, bumping my leg. Turning toward him, I realized he might be the best to start with.

"What are your plans now that you're not going to be working at the clinic?"

"No, clue. It's kind of exciting. I've always had a plan, and for the first time, I'm just playing it by ear." He shrugged. "For now, I'm going to help Slade out here. What about you?"

"I'm still looking, but I think I found something. I'm just not sure. It would mean—"

"Fish. Your turn."

"What?" I gasped, turning to gape at Slade. This hadn't been in the plan. "I thought it was just Lennox? How are you done already?"

Slade smirked, but didn't say anything as he stood up. Lenn smiled, moving off the chair, and taking the seat Slade had been in. I guess she was going to do it.

"It won't be bad, I promise."

Sitting down in the chair, she grabbed my hand, taking the gun Slade handed to her. "Lay your hand flat on the surface and don't move."

Nodding, I watched Slade as she inked me. He had a smirk on his face, arms crossed as he stood behind her, watching her work. I didn't know what his look meant, and it confused me. A few minutes later, she finished, and I looked down. That hadn't taken long at all. It was similar to the one she'd done on Slade, with lemons instead of stars. I grinned, warmth filling me.

"I love it."

"Welcome to the club, Simon Fisher. I'm inked on your skin forever."

Smiling, I nodded, butterflies filling me. "Do I get to see yours?"

Lennox nodded, lifting her shirt. There were two. The one on her heart was the symbol I'd come to know well, the heart on fire with wings. It was the one on the side of her ribs that caught my breath. It was beautiful and celestial, a perfect representation of Lennox. I'd never realized how perfect until I saw it on her. The ink almost glimmered as she moved, the crescent moon and lotus flower looked like they always belonged on her.

"Wow, babe. Those are beautiful." Slade snorted, but I could tell he appreciated the compliment, even if he wouldn't admit it.

"Zane, your turn."

"Me?" he squeaked, almost as shocked as I'd been.

Lennox smiled at him, patting the chair, so I hopped up. I squeezed his shoulder as I passed, taking my place back on the couch. Slade followed me, sitting close.

"You think she likes it?" he asked. Nodding, I grabbed his hand, turning to him.

"She loved it. It's perfect. You outdid yourself. I'm not just saying that either."

"I just want her first tattoo to be the best."

"It is because you gave it to her."

"Thank you." He leaned his forehead against mine, and I smiled, loving that this gruff man sought me out to ask things and wanted me to reassure him.

"Always, babe. I love you, even when you're a possessive alphahole."

"I think what you meant was, especially, when I'm possessive."

"Nope, I said what I mean." Laughing, we turned when Lennox said she was done with Thane's. He showed us the bass cleft heart with three music notes. I loved how they were all unique, but connected, showing our bond.

"Let's clean up and head home," Slade said. Every time he said home, it made my insides quiver.

"Wait, I need Lenn to find a spot for this." I reached into my pocket, pulling out the item I'd snagged earlier. Lenn laughed, grabbing it and placed the crumpled box of lemon drops on a shelf next to a picture of all of us.

"Why is a box of movie candy up there?" Thane asked, standing.

"It was the first time Lennox admitted she wanted to tattoo. Her first one is on the back."

"Don't look, it's awful! But it's the sentimental aspect that I love. Thanks, Si. Now, home?" Her eyes were telling me she had plans for something.

"There's one more thing I wanted to talk to you all about," I started, figuring I had nothing to lose.

The door chime went off, stopping me this time, and we all turned in shock. The shop wasn't open yet, so there shouldn't be anyone coming in at this time of night. Maybe it was Bubba stopping by to check it out.

Yet, when we stepped out to the lobby, it was to find a young girl, only confusing us more.

"Can we help you? We're not open yet." Lennox asked, her southern charm coming through since Slade had only glared at the girl.

"Are you Lennox?"

"I am."

"Oh, thank god, I've been trying to track you down."

We all stiffened, and she quickly went into repair mode. "No, sorry, poor choice of words. You see, Babs was my grandmother. We saw the news a few months back about everything that happened to you, and my gran," she paused, swallowing, "she told me to find you and give you this when she passed."

Her eyes had started to water by the end, and Lennox walked over to her, pulling the girl into a hug, her own eyes leaking at the news.

"I'm so sorry to hear that. She was a kind woman. She helped me find my way one day."

"I know. She told me all about the girl she met at her spot." The girl said, wiping her eyes. "You were a bright spot for her, and she talked about you often during those last months. I think it was the last trek she'd made up there, so it stuck." She took a deep breath, wiping her eyes more as Lennox held onto her arms. "Sorry, it's still so hard, knowing she's gone. Ugh," she said, waving a hand in front of her face to dry the tears. "Anyway, here, I feel like I might get closure now that I've finished Gran's last wish."

She thrust an envelope into Lenn's hands, turned, and left as quick as she'd come.

"What is it, Lenn? And who's Babs?" I asked.

She opened the envelope, ignoring my question as she pulled out a letter. Her eyes went wide the more she read it, a few gasps leaving her. Slade couldn't handle not knowing any longer and stalked over, preparing to grab it.

Lennox's head snapped up when he was a few feet away, but it wasn't in annoyance but excitement. She glanced at the three of us, a question on her lips.

"Anybody feel like going on a road trip?"

Chapter Five

THE LETTER

Dearest Lennox,

You might not remember me, but the day we met up on that hill is one that has played over and over in my head ever since. In fact, it was the last time I ever made it up there, so I was glad I got to share it with you.

They tell me that my health is failing and I won't have much longer to live. I don't know how much I buy into it, but they're the doctors. Of course, they might be onto something since I'm not even able to write this letter to you. My arthritis has taken my hands from me to the point that I can barely even hold a spoon. If I have to be fed by someone, I'm going to wish it was time to go. That, to me, feels like the most significant loss. It truly is a crime of dying to feel like your whole body is against you.

My nurse is telling me to get on with the purpose of this letter, so I suppose I shall go back to my point of writing it. You made an impression on me, young lady. Something about you inspired me and reminded me of my younger self. It made me think of all the things I enjoyed with my lovers.

When I saw you on the news, I was glad to see that your troubles looked to be over, and I hoped you'd found your happy ending. But just in case you needed a push, I thought of a brilliant way to help us both out.

So, as one rebel to another, I wondered if you could do a favor for me? When I go, I'd like to be remembered for how I lived and not the stuff they will write about me. Do you remember that story I told you about one of my lovers? The summer before I was to marry, he took me on an epic road trip where I got to try new foods, visit new places, and meet different people. It was my last hurrah, and I wish I'd been brave enough to choose him in the end. But that's in the past.

I'd like you to visit new places and experience the joy and freedom I wasn't allowed back then, with the men you love. I'll even give you a list of some ideas. In each city that you stop in, I want you to do something that scares you, something new, and something fun. If you complete them all, then not only will I have been honored how I wanted, but you just might find a little surprise within yourself you never thought possible.

I hope you choose to take the adventure. There's a whole world out there waiting for you on the open road.

Your hillside friend and fellow rebel,

Babs

List of places or things I recommend doing:

The Arch

Graceland

An Aquarium

Eat something new

Hear a band

Dance without reservation

Pet some animals

Do something only locals know

Climb a mountain

Visit five states

"ANYBODY FEEL like going on a road trip?" I asked as my alpha-hole lover descended on me. He reached out to take the letter, but I quickly moved it behind my back. Sticking out my tongue, I sidestepped from his reach.

"Nuh-uh. Answer the question first," I said, not giving in to his smolder. Stupid Slade and his stupid smolder.

Growling at not getting his way, he closed his eyes, taking a deep breath. Simon and Zane looked at me from the booth with curiosity on their faces. They both walked closer, and I suddenly felt like a trapped animal with no escape as the three of them cornered me.

"Babs was a kindred spirit I met that day I ran

from you two at the diner. That morning you first met Darcie," I said, hoping they'd settle if I gave them some information. "She's the one who told me to give you a chance to explain."

Swallowing, I searched the three men looking at me as they tried to decipher my question. Slade stopped, thinking through the information as he studied me. "What does she have to do with a road trip?"

"She wants me to remember her by experiencing new things. She's given me some tasks to honor her. It sounds fun, and I'd like to do it. She was a sweet old lady who reminded me that love was worth fighting for. Besides, after everything we've been through, don't we owe ourselves a vacation? I think it could be just what we need."

I lifted a shoulder, dropping my eyes. Suddenly, I felt nervous and like everything I'd just said was dumb. Feet came into view right before a tattooed finger lifted my chin.

"Is this something you want to do, Peach?"

I nodded, searching his eyes. Slade grunted, and I knew he wanted more.

"Yes," I said, licking my lips. When he went all-dominating on me, it always made me want to comply, even if I pushed his buttons most of the time.

He peered over his shoulder, but I was too worried to follow his line of sight and focused on the lotus flower tattoo on his neck that I now realized looked like the one he'd just given me.

"Your tattoo," I murmured, just as he turned his head back to me. His eyes lit with fire as he spotted where I was staring.

"Took you long enough, Peach." Slade smirked as he watched me, his eyes growing hungrier the more I stared back. It made me wonder if he was about to eat me, and I was willing to let him.

"Road trip?" Simon asked, moving closer. "That might actually work with what I've found." His voice was hesitant, pulling me from my lust fog with Slade, and I turned to him.

"What did you find?" I asked, then peered around and realized I'd been pressed up against the wall by Slade. Which, I'd admit, was one of my favorite places to be pressed up against him, but now was so not the time. "Actually, let's move this conversation to the coffee shop. I could use a coffee and muffin."

Slade groaned, laying his head against the wall, but sighed and stepped back, giving me some space. He grabbed Simon's hand and pulled him along, leaving Zane and me to lock up. Once the door and its million locks were engaged, Zane threw his arm around my shoulder as we followed the duo ahead of us down a few stores to Common Grounds, the coffee shop.

When we entered, the smell of coffee beans, sugar, and baked goods filled the air, and I took a deep breath, letting it fill my lungs. "Ah, yeah, that's the good stuff." I giggled, peeking over at Zane as he took in the place.

"This place is amazing," he said, a huge smile spreading across his face.

Tugging him toward the counter, I was excited to introduce him to Mrs. Patty. Simon already had her swooning as he complimented her, while Slade stood with his arms crossed, not saying a word. I swear, sometimes he asked people to spit in his drinks with his attitude.

"Lennox!" Mrs. Patty exclaimed, stepping out from behind the counter. She waddled over to me, lifting me up into her arms for a hug before I could blink. She rocked back and forth, squeezing me more. Wrapping my arms around her, I sank into her embrace.

"I should tan your hide for making an old woman scared!" she huffed, pulling back and checking me over. "At least you finally opened your eyes to the yummy men in your life." Lifting her eyebrows, she gave me a big smile. "Speaking of, introduce me to your new one."

She dropped my arms and turned to Zane, standing next to me. Before he could say anything, she grasped his cheeks and squeezed them. "Hmm, yeah, I can see the resemblance to the grouchy one. You're better looking, though." She winked, knowing that Slade could hear her, making Zane chuckle.

"Hey," he grumbled before Simon could soothe him.

"It's nice to meet you, Mrs. Patty. Lennox has told me all about your wonderful coffee creations. I can't wait to try one."

"Hmm, flattery. Yes, I like this one. You have permission to woo my girl then." She patted his cheek and returned to the counter, resuming her position behind the espresso machine.

"I'll remember that when you need someone to help unload your coffee beans," Slade huffed, scowling.

"Oh, Slade, you know I love you. I just have to make it fair. Now, don't be a party pooper. You ready for your greeting card wisdom of the day?"

"Yes!" I cheered, stepping closer. Slade rolled his eyes, but smiled.

"Yeah, yeah. Give it to us. It makes Peach happy."

"You know what you should do when life gives you lemons?" she asked, making Simon chuckle.

"Let me guess, make lemonade?"

"Nope," she said with a smug smile. "Throw them at your enemies."

We all stood there, our mouths agape, for a few seconds before we burst out into laughter.

"Okay, Mrs. Patty, you're even better than Lennox said," Zane said, wiping his eyes free of tears.

"Where did you learn that one?" I asked, leaning against the surface.

"My grandkids taught it to me. Good one, isn't it?" she asked, sliding four cups across the counter. "Now, y'all going to try some of my cobblers today?"

"If it's what I smelled when I walked in, then yes, please!"

"Good. I'll be right back."

Simon and Slade took the four cups of coffee over to a table while Zane and I waited for Mrs. Patty to return. When she brought out a steamy tray of cobbler with ice cream on top, my mouth began to water as I took in the desert.

"Oh, Mrs. Patty, this looks divine." She beamed as we paid, telling us to be good as she returned to the kitchen area.

There were two other customers in the coffee shop

and one additional employee, but they were all in their own little worlds as they worked on whatever they were doing. Sitting down at the booth with the tray, I slid the plate off eagerly and picked up the spoon. We all took a few bites of the warm cobbler as the ice cream melted, and before I knew it, it was gone.

"That was the best blackberry cobbler I've ever had," Zane proclaimed, sitting back to pat his stomach.

"You should try the peach. It's my favorite."

"I know of another peach that's still better," Slade cooed from across the booth. Instantly, my insides heated up, and I picked up my coffee to try to hide my reaction.

"So, what idea did you have, Simon?" I asked, turning my attention to him. Carefully, I shifted my legs, my pussy throbbing with need from one look.

"Well, I've been feeling pretty aimless and not sure what direction I wanted to go. Going back to the salon didn't feel right, and I can't hang around Tattooed Hearts forever either."

"Sure you can," Slade disagreed, sipping his coffee. "How else am I going to keep track of both of you?"

"As cute as that is," Simon stated, patting Slade's leg under the table, "I need my own thing. And

Thane is looking for something too. It's not just about me."

"What do I have to do with it?" he asked, practically licking his plate clean.

"Well, I was scrolling through LiveIt when I saw an ad. Have you ever heard of Sink-Ink-Think?"

Scrunching my nose, I rolled the words around in my head, trying to place them. "No, I can't say I have. What is it?" I asked, taking another gulp of the liquid gold.

"It sounds dumb," Slade interjected. "SIT? What, are we dogs now?"

Simon rolled his eyes but didn't let Slade's grumpiness at not being in the know deter him. "It started as a convention and has developed into this huge thing. It's now part convention with booths and tables and part competition. I think we should do it."

"Do it, how exactly?" I ask, not understanding his excitement.

"There are booths for hair, makeup, tattoos, and even some karaoke contests. It just seemed like a fun idea. Forget I mentioned it," Simon said, dropping his eyes. I could hear the hurt in his voice, and I knew we hadn't responded the way he wanted.

"Babe, it's not that I don't want to do it. I'm just trying to figure out what it is. You've had a few hours to look into it, and I can see you're excited about it. Let us get there before you decide for us."

"So, what you're saying is we'd tattoo people, do Lennox's letter thing, and you'd style hair?" Slade asked, peering at Simon until he lifted his head.

"Yeah."

"What about Thane?" Slade asked, looking at his brother. It made me happy he wasn't dismissing his place in our relationship. They'd come a long way since Nashville.

Simon looked over at him. "I thought it would be a good chance to find your passion. You talked about being excited about the possibilities. You could take photos, be our assistant, or even try writing. I want you with us. I didn't mean for it to sound like you weren't included."

Zane nodded, scratching his jaw as he thought it over. He looked over at me and then at Slade. "You know, we could make a trip to see Dad while we're traveling. And I have always wanted to take photos. It could be my thing. If nothing else, I could man the social media account for the shop."

Slade held his brother's eyes as he breathed deeply, finally closing them as he nodded. "Fine. If we can make it work with Peach's thing, then the SHIT thing could work too. We'll see about Dad."

"It's SIT," Simon said, laughing. "But, thank you."

"So, road trip? Oh, this is going to be a blast. Just me, a van, and my three best guys."

"Wait, a van?" Slade asked, looking at me.

"Would you prefer a camper?"

"I'll take care of the vehicles. You three start mapping out our journey. Where do we head first for Babs?" he asked.

"St. Louis, Missouri."

Chapter Seven

SLADE

SIGNING the last of the papers, I slid the cash across the table to the guy. He quickly flitted through it, counting, but it was all there. When he was satisfied, he passed me the keys. Thankfully, I'd made some connections last fall when I'd been looking for a replacement car for Peach. So when she said we needed a van, I knew exactly where to go.

It just sucked that it was a few hours away, keeping me from my girl. The smile on her face when she saw me drive up in this thing would be worth it, though.

Opening the back, I laid down the seats and eyed the carpet. If I rolled my motorcycle up into it, it would stain it, not to mention I'd need to pull them out to get her to fit. Scrubbing my face, I debated on what to do. I should've taken Simon up on his offer to tag along, but it had been something I'd selfishly wanted to do myself.

"I could make you an offer, I reckon," the man said, eyeing me.

Lifting my eyebrow, I assessed him. "I'm not selling my bike."

He laughed, the sound hearty as he slapped his knee. "What would I need your bike for out here?"

Sighing, I knew he had a point. It had been difficult driving the last few miles on that bumpy road. "What do you suggest?" I shielded my eyes from the sun while waiting for him to answer.

"Well, I could sell you a tarp, but getting those seats out would be hell just so it would fit. So, I'll do you one better."

Crossing my arms, I ground my back molars as I waited for him to get to the point. Southerners always had all the time in the world.

"Yeah?" I finally asked when he didn't look like he would spill unless I prompted him. Hell, he could've fallen asleep up on his porch for all I knew.

He slapped his knee again, getting up from the rickety rocking chair that had seen better days. The old man climbed down the steps, dodging broken bird baths that had all seemed to pile up on one side of his yard, and moved to the other, where it was full of rusted car parts, old bathtubs, and what looked to be a horse trailer. It was dented on one side, so it was hard to tell. The old man slapped the trailer I'd been looking at, smiling at me like it made sense.

"You want me to buy a horse trailer? It looks… bent." I knew I needed to tread carefully with my words, but the thing looked to be on its last legs.

"It's not a horse trailer, it's a pony one, and yeah, it's busted on this side, but that makes it perfect for what you need." He grinned wide, his yellow teeth showing as he waited for me to be excited. I was beginning to wonder if he stole the van I purchased, with how ridiculous he was being.

"But I don't have a horse. I have a motorcycle," I said slowly, like it shouldn't be that easy to mix the two up.

The man slapped his leg again, laughing at me as he pointed. "You're a funny kid. Of course you don't have a horse. That would be dumb. You wouldn't want to put a horse in here."

I stared, hoping it would make sense if I just stayed quiet. It did not.

"Okay, I give up. How will this help me?" I asked, rubbing the back of my neck. I decided I was ready to leave loony town and return to Peach and Simon.

"I reckon your bike will fit perfectly in the stall. About the same length as a pony, and you only need one side. Winner, winner." He grinned wide like he'd just solved the world's hardest puzzle.

Walking over, I peered into the trailer, realizing he was right. It might be weird, but it would work.

"Fine. How much?"

A few hundred dollars later and with his help to hitch and load my bike onto the trailer, I was headed back home. Sitting behind the van's wheel, I turned the dial of the radio, realizing it didn't get great reception. We'd have to fix that. Giving up when it would only play polka music, I settled in for the drive, thoughts of how I could take both Simon and Lennox in this van to christen it filling my head.

Yeah, this was going to be good.

Despite my brother tagging along and us having to do a bunch of silly competitions, it would be fun to travel. I knew Lennox hadn't done much of it, so I was excited about getting to share the world outside of Bowling Green, Kentucky with her.

If I had to do a few tattoos along the way, I guess it wasn't too horrible. It would be good for business as we got the shops back up and running. I could even see if there would be a good location for a third one.

The whole time I was planning, I conveniently left out visiting my father and his new girlfriend. Hopefully, Thane would forget about it as well.

"I'M ALMOST HOME. Can you bring Peach outside and cover her eyes?"

"Yep, can do."

"Thanks, Si."

"See you in a few."

He hung up the phone, and I couldn't deny how excited I was to show her. It amazed me that I'd been able to deny having her for so long. I'd been punishing myself more than anyone those two years. I was glad it was all in the past now. I couldn't imagine living my life without both her and Simon and even my twin. He'd been a happy gain to reclaim back in my life.

So, why are you avoiding your father? my subconscious whispered, but I quickly ignored it and shoved it away.

Pulling into the driveway, I spotted Simon and Thane standing with Peach. Simon had his hands over her eyes, and I could see her bouncing, her luscious curves moving with the motion. Yeah, I was so going to christen this van later. Her thighs begged to be claimed as I ate her out on the hood, the back-seat, and maybe even the roof. With Lennox, it was never enough.

The trailer whined behind me as I slowed to a stop, and I had to remember to give myself more space to maneuver it around. What in the world was I going to do with the damn thing now? That would have to wait because the only thing I could focus on at the moment was Peach.

Turning off the engine, I opened the door and stepped into the grass. Walking around to the front, I leaned against it, smirking. "Take a look, Peach."

Simon dropped his hands, but Lennox kept her eyes shut, peeking a little. "You're not going to be dressed as a clown, right? Because I'm not responsible for my knee-jerk reaction to attack all clowns if you are."

Laughing, I dropped my smirk and walked forward, taking her hands. "No clowns, Peach. Just look. I promise you'll love it."

The guys also encouraged her, giving her the bravery to open her eyes fully. I watched her the whole time as she took in the bright turquoise VW van I'd been able to find. It had a little wear and tear, but the brakes and tires were new, so at least we'd be good on that front.

A shriek left her as she finally accepted it was real, her hands covering her mouth before she turned and jumped into my arms. I caught her easily, her plush body fitting against me nicely. Lifting her up by her ass, she wrapped her legs around my waist as I carried her over to it.

Peach leaned back, looking at me with awe in her eyes. "I can't believe you did this. I thought you hated them."

"But you love them, and I love you, so I did it to make you happy. That's all I want. Well, a blow job every day doesn't hurt either." Smirking, I anticipated the slap she delivered as I set her down next to the door. The other two guys were already walking around and inspecting the van.

"Did you get me a pony?" Simon asked, winking as he took in the trailer.

"Long story, but it was the best solution to getting the bike home. How is the trip planning going on your end?"

"Great!" Lennox chirped. "I think if we make some lists of everything we need tonight, then we should be able to pack and set off tomorrow. I need to say goodbye to my parents and Bubba. Oh, and Darcie." She started walking back toward the house, continuing to talk and list things off as she walked.

"If she wasn't so cute, I'd be worried," Thane said. Staring up at him, I shook my head.

"That makes no sense. Her cuteness subtracts logic?" I asked, staring at my brother like he'd hit his head.

"Makes sense to me." He shrugged as he continued following her, and I shook my head, turning back to the trailer.

Simon waited at the back end and helped me pull the motorcycle off. Together, we rolled it into the detached garage, and I kicked out the kickstand, rolling it to a stop. Taking a few seconds, I wiped her down and patted the seat as I realized it might be some time before I got to ride her again. Looking up, I spotted Simon staring at me with a soft smile.

"You'll be okay, babe. I doubt you'll even miss her."

Snorting, I turned and leaned against my bike, taking him in. His silver-gray hair swooped over, highlighting his gray eyes. His face was clean-shaven, and he stood watching me in a pair of slim jeans, Converse, and a band tee. Simon had a style that was effortless and yet was always in fashion. Bringing my hand to my mouth, I tugged on my lip as my gaze lazily dragged down him.

"Mmm, you know, maybe you should give me a good memory with my bike, so I have it to look back on."

"Oh, yeah?" he asked, his lip curling up on the side. "And what kind of memory would this be?"

"I have a few in mind," I said, my hand dropping down to my jeans. His eyes followed, watching every move as I slowly lowered the zipper. Watching him, I saw when his breathing increased and he licked his lips. Simon tilted forward, his feet already yearning to bring him closer.

Between the look on his face and the feel of Peach against me earlier, my cock had no problem getting on board with the plan. Lowering my pants just enough, I freed myself and began to stroke my dick as it hardened.

The sight of my cock in my hand was all it took for Simon to bolt forward, taking it from me as he dropped to his knees and gave me a long lick. Bracing my hands back on my bike seat, I spread my legs to provide myself with a better position by widening my stance.

Weaving my fingers through Simon's silver locks, I kept the pressure soft for now as he began to work me over, licking and sucking up and down my length.

"Yes, fuck, Si." Moaning, my head fell back as I let him set his pace as he continued to suck the living daylights out of me. When his hand reached down and began to fondle my balls, I knew I wouldn't last much longer. Pulling the strands harder now, I peered down at my lover as he took my cock between his lips, the sight almost making me unload on him.

"Take it all, Si. Fuck." Tugging his hair, I gave him just enough pressure to follow my command as he swallowed, opening his throat more so that he took me all the way into his mouth and down his throat. It was too much, and I came hard, spilling my cum as I roared out my release.

Panting, I let go of his hair, smoothing it in place as he slowly released me from his lips. Standing, he pulled me to him, kissing me long and hard.

"How's that for a memory?" he asked, wearing a shit-eating grin.

"Yeah, I think that will do just fine."

"Come on. We better help pack before Lenn makes us start to color coordinate."

Panic crossed my face as I quickly zipped up my pants and grabbed his hand. "Shit, you're so right. I'm not going to wear all blue again."

Simon snickered at my expense, remembering our ill-fated Halloween costumes, but he followed along, making my heart full.

I might complain about missing my bike, but I'd give it up forever if it meant I got to do life with them. Lennox and Simon were my forever, stupid van and all.

Chapter Eight

KISSING my brother on the head one last time, I promised my parents to give them calls and texts every few days on our progress. I'd almost made it out the door when my dad pulled me back into his arms, hugging me tight again.

"Be careful, pumpkin. I trust Slade, Simon, and Thane, but be careful."

"I will, Dad. You know they won't let anything happen to me."

He huffed, making a noise before kissing my forehead and finally letting me go. Taking the chance, I stepped outside as quickly as possible, so I wouldn't be pulled back into another hugfest. Thankfully, Bubba had only required two hugs before he let us go, promising to look after the shop. It felt weird leaving it, but I knew that sometimes you couldn't let chances pass you by or you'd miss them, and this felt like one of those moments.

Zane leaned against the van, having escaped my parents much quicker. Stepping into his waiting arms, I leaned against his chest, just listening to his heart in the warm air. A door shut, and I peered over, watching Simon and Slade as they left Si's parents' house. They were carrying bags of goodies, and I laughed, knowing they hadn't made it out without a mountain of food. What was it with southern moms that they had to load you up before you went on any trip?

"Does any of that need to be cold?" Zane asked.

"Yeah, some," Simon sighed. "I told her we didn't have room."

"Might need to get a second cooler, not that we have much room to put one," Slade said, huffing as he opened the back and looked into it with all our bags and totes full of supplies. "We should've gone with the RV. We have no room for all of our stuff."

"It'll be fine. Just put the cold food up front so we can eat it first," I said, letting go of Zane and opening the side door. I made a few adjustments, bending over as I shoved things under the seats. When I peeked back up, I found all three staring at my bum.

Laughing, I shook my butt a little, enjoying their stares on me, and they looked up, one by one, to meet my eyes. The heat reflected back at me never got old, and I momentarily debated stopping back at home and having a quickie. The sun shining in my eyes reminded me that we wanted to get to St. Louis before it was too late. With a four-hour drive ahead of us, it was best to get on the road since it was already mid-afternoon.

"Keep those thoughts for later, but I think it's best to get headed on our journey. Who's driving first?" I asked, looking between all of them.

Slade rolled his eyes like I'd asked a stupid question and pulled the keys out of his pocket. He walked over to the driver's side and got in, not answering. Simon rolled his too, but smiled as he grabbed my hand and pulled me into the backseat with him, leaving Zane to sit up front with his brother. It was quiet as the journey began, and Slade took the ramp onto the interstate.

"This will be the first time I've ever been anywhere outside of Kentucky or Tennessee," I said, watching the hills blur as they sped by.

"Well, Slade and I are pros at checking out the hotspots. Between Babs' list, the competitions, and our own curiosity, I think we'll be able to have some fun," Zane affirmed, smiling at me.

"I'm excited. I've only been to Florida with my grandparents, which wasn't the best trip. So, to travel as an adult and do what we want sounds heavenly," Simon piped in, squeezing my hand. It had been our dream to travel together growing up, and now we were getting to. I guess I owed it to Babs for making it happen.

"Now that we're on the road properly, we need some road trip music," Zane stated, pulling out his phone. Slade had informed us that the radio was busted, but I'd had a Bluetooth adapter that plugged into the auxiliary outlet allowing us to play whatever we wanted over the van's speaker system.

Music began playing, a fun and upbeat tune, making me want to dance. So I did. Simon laughed as I twisted to and fro, raising my hands in the air. When the lyrics started, I began to sing along, no longer feeling shy about singing in front of people. Simon began to sing with me, and we made up our own dance as we shimmied our shoulders to the beat. When the song ended, we fell against one another, laughing.

"You're not too bad, Si, but Peach, you gotta enter one of those contests. I love listening to you sing," Slade said from the front.

Catching his eyes in the rearview, I saw the sincerity. Some of the old panic at singing in front of others who could judge me began to crawl up my throat, and I shook my head.

"No, I like just singing for fun. I've accepted that about myself. Let's leave it at that."

Something in Slade's eyes told me he wouldn't be dropping this anytime soon, so I turned and looked out the window. Pulling out a journal, I read the letter again and looked over the map as I jotted down some of the places to visit in St. Louis.

"Where's the first competition?" I asked Si as I began to make an itinerary.

"It's in Branson, Missouri, which is about four-ish hours, I believe, from St. Louis."

"When do we need to be there?" Simon had taken care of all the logistics with the promoters, telling them we'd sign up for a few of the shows as we went along. They were willing to accommodate us due to Slade's notoriety in the tattoo world.

"Registration's in two days, so we'll have tonight and all day tomorrow in St. Louis, but will need to leave the next morning for Branson."

Nodding, I wrote down the time as I began to search for things, along with items on Bab's list to do, and jotted them down. I began to read out some of the options with the guys picking one thing they wanted to do. When I had five things, I figured it was enough if we wanted to really be able to enjoy any of them.

. . .

1. The Arch
    2. Anheuser-Busch
    3. City Garden
    4. Grant's Farm
    5. Moto Museum

EXCITEMENT TO DO it all coursed through me, but I knew I needed to pace myself so I wasn't worn out before we got to the end of the trip.

A little while later, we crossed the state line into Indiana, adrenaline pumping through me that we were really doing this. I leaned against Simon, watching out his window, taking in the view.

"We're doing it, Si," I said, sighing wistfully.

"Yeah, we are." He dropped a kiss down onto my head, squeezing me to him. He was comfortable, so I closed my eyes and drifted off to sleep.

A bit later, I was jostled awake. "Lenn, we're crossing into Illinois. I thought you'd want to know."

Sitting up, I wiped the sleep from my eyes and took in the new state as we passed the sign. "Wow, this state is busy," I said, noticing the barely moving traffic.

"Yeah, there's a wreck up ahead. I'm going to pull off at the next exit so I can stretch my legs. If someone else wants to drive, they can," Slade said, switching lanes as he did what he said.

The need to pee hit me, and I climbed out with the others and headed into the gas station while Zane filled the van with gas. My eyes took everything in, trying to catalog the difference between here and Kentucky.

"It's a gas station, Peach. They're all basically the same. You'll see differences soon. Come on."

Slade tugged me down the hall to the restrooms, and we both headed in. Quickly, I held my nose, trying not to touch anything. It seemed the gas station's level of cleanliness was something else that stayed the same. Yuck.

Using a paper towel to open the door, I found Slade waiting for me. Keeping the door open with my foot, I tossed the paper towel back into the trash as he laughed.

"What?" I asked. He shook his head in lieu of answering, kissing me as we walked, and I veered toward the snacks.

We didn't need any more snacks since we were full on food, but the lure of candy and a cold drink pulled me in. Scanning the shelves, I searched for something new to jump out, but nothing was calling to me. Sighing, I gave up and headed to the counter where Slade was paying for the gas.

When he turned around, he placed a cap on my head that I hadn't noticed him buying. Pulling it off, I read the inscription *"Illi-noice."* Laughing, I set it back on my head and pulled my hair behind my ears.

"And here I thought *'Getting lucky in Kentucky'* was lame."

Simon scowled at the hat when we got back into the van, muttering about its damage to my hair. I ignored him, used to his high maintenance standards. Slade climbed into the bench seat with me, pulling me practically into his lap as we started our journey again.

I got lost drawing some sketches in my journal as we drove, the wreck having been cleared up by the time we got back on the interstate. So when we neared Missouri, I hadn't realized we were almost there. Slade nudged me as we passed the state sign and then pointed to the Arch in the distance.

"Wow, it's beautiful at night," I said. The sun was setting, and the lights were beginning to come on as we made our way to the hotel. Thirty minutes later, we pulled into the parking garage of our downtown hotel, and we all got out and stretched. Slade went to check us in while we began to sort the things we needed out of the back and leave the things we didn't. We covered them up with a blanket when we were done and hoped no one would break into the van while we were away. Thankfully, the garage was monitored, so we hoped it would be enough. Nobody wanted to lug Simon's hair products to a million different places if we didn't have to.

"I was thinking the van needs a name," I said as we began to head toward the hotel.

"Hmm, what do you think goes with that color?" Zane asked, tugging a bag onto his shoulder.

"I don't know if it has to be color connected. Maybe it could be Babs since she's leading us."

"It has merit, but I don't know if I can sex you up in Babs, and I plan to sex you up, so your call," Slade said as he joined us, taking a bag from me.

Laughing, we walked into the hotel, taking the elevator up to our floor. When we stepped into our room a few minutes later, I was amazed at its size. I hadn't stayed in many hotel rooms, but this seemed bigger than most.

"It's a suite," Slade said, answering the question on my face. "But the best part..." he trailed off, walking over to the window and opening the curtains, "is the view."

Gasping, I took in the lights that were now lit up on the Arch in full view from our room. "It's magnificent."

When the guys joined me and I took in our reflection against the Arch, and I knew that this trip, this journey, would do as Babs said. It would change our foundation into something extraordinary. This push she'd given me was a gift I never would've dreamed of having. Making a vow to myself, I promised to take every opportunity presented to us on this voyage and follow her instructions of doing some-thing scary, something new, and something fun, no matter how terrifying it might be.

It was time for this baby bird to spread her wings.

Chapter Nine

IN FRONT OF THE GROUP, the brewmaster waxed poetically about how beer was made, but all I could think about was the next part. When Lenn had asked us what we wanted to do, we suggested something fun that intrigued us in the city, and I knew I wanted to come meet the horses. It worked out that it also lined-up with Slade's curiosity about brewing beer.

I just hadn't planned on having to do an hour-and-a-half tour of the place before I got to see the Clydesdales. Lennox shuffled next to me, looking at her phone just as much as me. We were both ducking out of this one to go to ours while the brothers carried on.

"Is it time?" she whispered, looking up at me with hope in her eyes.

Slade huffed next to me but nodded, only taking

his eyes off the man up front to give me a look. I read everything it said, though.

Watch her. Don't let her out of your sight. Her safety is in your hands.

Okay, so maybe that was a little long-winded for Slade, but it was about the gist of it. Lennox didn't know that since her stalker, Slade had become even more of a bear in regards to her safety. I couldn't blame him, though. We'd almost lost her. That wasn't a world I wanted to live in.

Taking her hand, I nodded to the twins and headed back to the entrance with Lennox. Our steps were quick as we eagerly made our way to the next tour.

"I'm so excited," she said, practically skipping in her Chucks as she danced along next to me.

Squeezing her hand, I directed us to the front of the gathered crowd for this tour. I had to say, I was impressed with Anheuser-Busch's system. They had four different tours of the brew facility and stables, depending on what you wanted to see and learn. If I liked beer, I might've been more inclined to learn how it was made, but since it was just something I barely tolerated, it was the Clydesdales that drew me in.

"Welcome, everyone! We're about to set off on our tour of the stables and learn all about these beautiful creatures. First up, a few safety rules. Please do not travel off on your own. Stay with the group. And unless we say it's okay, do not touch any of the horses. While they are trained, no one wants to spook a horse. It isn't pretty what happens as a result. So, let's keep it safe and fun."

The small crowd hollered out their agreement, and we began to follow the tour guide toward the stables. It was still cool this early in the morning, and I rubbed my arms as we set off. Lennox had on a jean jacket over her dress, making her the smart one of the two of us.

The closer we got, the more we could smell and hear the horses. The shuffling of their hoofs on the ground and the smell of hay and manure greeted us as it filled the air.

"The Budweiser Clydesdales refers to teams of Clydesdale horses used to pull restored turn-of-the-century beer wagons for Budweiser. They first appeared in 1933, given as a gift to the brewery's CEO from his son to celebrate the repeal of prohibition," the tour guide started, motioning toward a stall where a beautiful brown horse was chewing hay.

Lennox gasped next to me, and I squeezed her hand, feeling the magic of the moment myself as we got to be part of these beautiful creatures' existence.

Looking around, I couldn't help but feel goosebumps on my skin at the historic brick and stained-glass stable around me. It was truly magical.

"… the stables were built in 1885 and house ten horses. Eight horses are driven at any time, but ten are on each team to provide alternates for the hitch when needed…."

"Si, look!" Lennox whispered-shouted, pointing to a horse at the front who was shaking his mane like he was in a hair commercial. She covered her mouth, laughing at the sight.

"To qualify for one of the hitches, a Budweiser Clydesdale must be a gelding with an even temperament and strong, draft horse appearance. They must be at least four years old, stand at least 18 hands when fully mature, and weigh between 1,800 and 2,300 pounds. In addition, each horse must be bay in color—have a reddish-brown coat with a black mane and tail, and have four white stocking feet and a blaze of white on the face."

"Wow, I never knew there was such a strict requirement. What about the horses that don't meet that? Are their dreams just ruined?" Lennox asked, looking up at me with her big eyes.

Pulling her into my arms, I moved over to the stall the horse attendant motioned us toward. "I'm sure there are other jobs for them, Lenn."

She sighed, letting it go for now. Together, we learned how to brush and groom one of the gentle giants over the next thirty minutes as they talked us through their routine, training regiment, and lifestyle.

"I think this horse has it better than me," Lennox said, laughing.

"Alright, folks. That's all for today. Please line up here if you want to take a selfie with one of our horses."

Lennox grabbed my hand and moved us toward where the guide pointed, making us the first in line. Together, we cheesed next to the horse as he sniffed and tolerated our presence.

Lennox kept looking at the picture on her phone as we walked back toward the front, where we were to meet the brothers. Slade saw us as we approached and sighed, knowing the look on her face.

"I'm not buying you a horse, Lennox."

She looked up, and I swear she had tears in her eyes. "That's rude. I wasn't going to ask for one." She strolled off, taking Thane's hand, and pulled him toward the van as Slade looked at me, giving me a look.

"She was." I nodded, smirking. "She was in heaven. If you ever screw up enough to need an epic 'I'm sorry' gift, well, you already have half a trailer to haul it," I joked, dodging his arm as he reached out to smack me. Laughing, we walked back together, ready to head to the rest of our activities for the day.

AFTER LUNCH at one of the places Thane had picked out, we made our way to the Moto Museum, where I feared we were about to find Slade in a drool coma as he looked at all the vintage motorcycles from over twenty different countries.

"And he made fun of me for the horses," Lennox hissed, finally drawing Slade's attention.

"Peach, the advantage of a motorcycle over a horse is it doesn't shit bigger than you." He lifted his eyebrows, making Lennox laugh, even if she would deny it.

"We should hit Citygarden now, before it gets too late," Thane said, looking at the time. Slade sighed, acting pained to leave the motorcycles, but eventually walked out, picking Lennox up as he did and throwing her up into his arms.

"Having fun?" I asked Thane as we followed them back to the van.

"Yeah. It's nice getting out and doing things with Slade like we used to."

"Any thoughts on what you want to do after our road trip?" I asked, sensitive to the topic since I seemed to have found myself in the same boat.

"Not yet. You?"

"Nope. Do you think 'lover boy' is a job title to aspire to?" I asked, laughing at the end.

"For some, it probably is."

Laughing, we climbed into the van and headed to the outdoor park, an urban oasis featuring modern and contemporary art, native plants, and six rain gardens. Walking through together, we saw a giant eyeball, a giant deer sculpture, and so many other natural and man-made sculptures; my brain was full of all the magnificent sights.

"This place is amazing!" Lennox beamed, spinning around with her arms open wide.

"Come on, I'm hungry. Let's grab some food, and then it should be time for our tram ride in the Arch," Slade said, pulling her toward a downtown restaurant.

None of us argued. The day had been fun but long, and I was famished. After a delicious meal, we headed toward the Arch, the sun beginning to set as we neared. Initially, we'd planned to do it first thing, but Lennox had changed her mind after seeing it lit up at night.

Standing in line, I shifted on my feet, the feeling

of being watched pricking me again. I'd felt it all day but assumed it was just my paranoia about being outside Kentucky with everything that had gone down last fall.

"What is it?" Slade asked, noticing my shuffling.

"Nothing." I shook it off, not wanting to put him on high alert for nothing.

Lennox peered back at me but turned toward the front when the clerk motioned. "We have four tickets reserved under Lennox James," she said, her southern charm shining through.

"Ah yes, Miss James. Here you go. There was also something left for you."

I looked to Slade, apprehension filling my gut. The lady handed Lennox her four tickets and slid across a familiar-looking envelope she retrieved from under her desk. Lennox picked it up, finding her name on the front.

"It must be from Babs," she breathed, looking up at us, her eyes big. "Should I open it now or wait?"

We moved away from the ticket line and went to stand in the tramline. It felt like herding a bunch of cattle to me. One line to the next.

"You might as well open it now. You've got the time," I said, motioning toward the hundred people in front of us.

Lennox nodded, opening the envelope and

pulling out the letter. The three of us watched as she read it, a smile crossing her face here and there as a tear tracked down her cheek. In the end, she nodded, a soft chuckle leaving her as she folded it back into the envelope.

"What did it say?" Slade asked, never able to wait.

"I'll tell you later. Not here."

Slade gritted his teeth, his nostrils flaring, but nodded. Wrapping my arm around his waist, I pulled him to me, hoping to help calm him down.

Thirty minutes later, the feeling of being watched was still with me; if anything, it felt even more intense. Shuffling, I kept peering around, trying to see if I could find the source. A pair of eyes landed on me, and I quickly looked away before remembering I was supposed to be seeing if they looked familiar. Glancing back, they were gone, and I chalked it up to nothing. Nothing in me clicked, so I figured it had just been a random tourist.

"Can you believe this Arch is 630 feet wide and 630 feet tall?" Lennox asked, looking up from the brochure she'd read while waiting.

"Don't remind me," Slade huffed, looking a little pale as he began to think about going up in the pod.

Our turn for the tram was up, and we climbed in. Slade sneered at the stranger who tried to board with us, not wanting to share the space. The pod was meant for five people, but we took up a lot of space between us three guys. But really, I think Slade didn't want anyone else to see him freaking out about the height.

Lennox held his hand, whispering things to him I wished I could hear as it seemed to work on distracting him. The pod rocked back and forth, and according to the little placard on the inside, the barrel rotated 155 degrees before switching to the next direction.

We were at the top four minutes later and stepped out onto the observation deck. Lennox wasted no time walking toward the window, looking out into the city. I followed, intrigued by how high up we were and how vast we could see.

"Babe, come look," I urged, finding Slade standing as far from the window as possible.

"I'm good right here," he said, clutching the wall. Smiling, I turned and held Lennox in my arms as we looked out at the landscape.

"I can't wait to sketch this. I want to remember it forever," she sighed. "This was what Babs was talking about. Finding beauty in the simple things."

A while later, I managed to drag Lennox away from the window, and we all got in line to head down. Standing there, I felt the hair on my neck grow as a scuffle in front of us broke out. Slade pulled Lennox into his arms as the guys began to shove in our direction, barely missing us. Slade growled at them, and Thane used his height to block them from our vantage point as they began to break up.

Security guards came over and escorted them both to the back elevator used for emergencies. Our time to head back down came a few moments later, and we stepped into the pod, the descent only taking us three minutes as the mechanics used gravity to rotate the barrels quicker. Stepping off the tram, Slade seemed to relax now that we were back on solid ground.

Lennox moved her bag, looking into it when she jerked up, searching for something. My hackles raised even more, and I began looking to, even though I didn't know what for.

"What is it, Lenn?"

"My wallet, it's gone. I think…" she trailed off as she searched the crowd. "There." She pointed to the two guys who'd been escorted by the security guards. They were being released from the little booth, both shoving off the arms of the guards.

Slade looked at me as she started to march toward them, not caring that they'd just been fighting 630 feet in the air. Thane got to her first, stopping her from running right up to the men.

"Lennox, what's going on?" he asked, as Slade and I caught up.

"Since when can you move that fast?" I asked, slightly out of breath.

"They took my wallet. It had to be them," she said, pointing. The two men saw us looking at them and took off, running out the door into the park.

"Fuck," Slade said before he took off after them. Thane looked at me, and I held my hands up, not inclined to chase people. I knew my strengths, and running was not one of them.

Taking Lennox's hand, she practically pulled me out the door as we searched for where they'd all run off. A few minutes later, we spotted Slade with his foot pressed to one of the guys on the ground. He nodded for us to come over, so we sprinted, eager to hear what they had to say.

"Give it to her," Slade ordered when we were within earshot.

"Sorry ma'am. No hard feelings. You should really watch your belongings better. We easily pinpointed you as a tourist."

Slade humphed, but then let the guy go once he returned Lennox's wallet. She briefly looked through it, satisfied when everything was there. Taking Lennox's other hand, we headed toward Thane, who was standing up ahead with a curious look on his face. I shook my head, trying to let him know it was okay. Though, I didn't know if I really believed that.

No one spoke as we approached the van, an eerie silence descending on us. Slade turned, something changing in his eyes as he glanced at Lennox.

"What did the letter say?"

Lennox bit her lip, shaking her head. "It was mostly about her time at the Arch and how she enjoyed seeing the city. She said she shared a kiss with one of her fellas at the top. Which I meant to do. Dang it!"

Lennox began to fidget with the hem of her dress, her classic tell that she wasn't sharing everything.

"What else, Lenn?" I asked, figuring it was better to get to the bottom of this.

Sighing, her shoulders dropped as she looked up, meeting all of our eyes. "Do you think I was targeted? Do I have a sign on me that says gullible? Why else do bad things seem to occur to me?"

She bit her lip, tears welling in her eyes, and I couldn't take it. I swept her into my arms, smoothing her hair down. I didn't want her to be scared to live life.

"That's it, we're going home," Slade said, turning around, his decision made.

"No! We can't let someone else rule our trip," I said sternly, zeroing on Slade. Thane stood to the side, uncertainty plaguing his features. Lennox patted me as she stepped back, standing between Slade and me.

"Simon's right. I just got nervous, but I don't want one bad thing to ruin this. This is the first time I've ever been away from home, and I love all the new experiences we've made. I don't want that to end."

Slade's hand tightened on the door handle as he peered out into the darkness of the parking lot. He took several deep breaths before he looked at her and gave an answer.

"Fine. But the moment it gets dangerous, I'm throwing you over my shoulder and walking back to our home if I have to."

Lennox nodded, leaning into me as Slade climbed into the van. "Why does that sound hot and like I sort of want to test him?" she asked, licking her lips.

Laughing, I pulled her to my side, and we settled into our seats. I made a commitment to myself to no longer ignore my gut feelings. Our safety, Lennox's life, could depend on it.

Chapter Ten

LENNOX

"AM I DREAMING?" I whispered when I felt hands begin to roam my body. I'd had too many vivid sex dreams to discount them.

"I hope not," a voice said from under the blankets a moment before I felt a hot mouth on my lower regions.

"Son of a bee sting!" I hissed, my body bucking up at the slight touch. The mouth did not relent, though, holding me down as he devoured me, and eventually, my body caught up and lowered back to the bed, a long, languid moan escaping me.

My hands gripped the sheets next to me as I yearned to grab hold of something, but it was still dark in the room, the curtains drawn, casting every-thing into darkness. I realized that there weren't any other bodies next to me as my hips bucked, and I tried to ride the wave whoever was beneath the covers was sending me on.

My brain woke up more as pleasure coursed through me, and I tried to figure out who it was. My money was on Simon. The twins both liked to get up early and work out, the masochists. They were more alike than they liked to admit sometimes.

When the person below began to swirl their tongue and plunge two fingers into me, I was a goner. The early morning surprise had my walls tightening as I began to spasm around their digits, and the sensation I'd only experienced once before rushed over me, and I orgasmed so hard, I squirted, dousing their face in my cum.

A loud moan of approval sounded before they began climbing up my body. When the blanket fell away, I was rewarded with the smiling face of my first love, Simon.

"Good morning, Si," I rasped, my body still waking up, my throat dry from my moan.

"Yes, it is," he said, grinning widely at me.

"You feel proud of yourself, don't you?" I asked, chuckling. I ran my fingers through his silver hair, the soft texture feeling nice against my fingers.

"Damn straight. I'm still the only one who's done that, right?" he asked, some of his confidence fading.

"Oh yeah, stud. That honor is all yours."

Giggling, I pulled him closer, kissing him as we rolled over to our sides. "Where're the other two?" I asked, hitching my leg over his side.

"Gym," he managed to breathe out between our kisses.

"So we have time to ourselves?" I asked, feeling him grow harder against me.

"Yes."

It was all I needed to hear as I pushed him over and straddled him. Leaning over, I took a second to adjust him at my entrance before sliding the rest of the way down. Bracing my arms against the headboard, I moved forward as my knees pressed into his sides. Simon gripped my hips, helping to pull me with each thrust. He let go with one hand and reached up, twisting my nipple before leaning forward and taking it into his mouth.

Moving my hands to his shoulders, I threw my head back, my hair falling against my skin as I picked up my speed, riding him like there was no tomorrow. Soon, Simon couldn't focus on anything other than holding onto me, his head thrown back as he moaned.

"I'm close," I managed to whisper, the sound hoarse.

"Me… too."

Thrusting forward, I rotated my hips as I clung to

his shoulders. Simon pulled me as far as I could go, holding me there as he began to fill me. His thumb reached down, swirling my clit in a circle, and I fell over the edge as I climaxed, my body going limp against his.

Panting, we both laughed as we stared at one another. "I definitely think I prefer to work out that way any day."

"Me too, Lemon Drop, me too." Grinning, we climbed out of the bed, and I stretched my muscles, a little sore from all the walking the day before.

"I guess we should shower and pack up. I want to hit Grant's Farm when it opens. Do you think we'll have time to visit the horses there too?" I asked, walking into the bathroom as Simon followed.

"It's a huge place, so it might depend on what we all want to see," Simon offered as I started the water.

"How do you feel about the competition? You haven't done hair in a while. I wasn't sure if you were still interested in it."

We stepped into the shower together, closing the glass door. Neither of us answered while we took turns standing under the water to wet our hair. Simon began to massage some shampoo into mine, never able to miss the opportunity to play with his favorite guinea pig.

"I love hair. I think I was just bored of the salon. It

wasn't challenging anymore. Outside of you and a few people who wanted to branch out color-wise, it was the same cut and style day in and day out. I want to do something more. SIT is a good chance for me to practice my skill and see what's cutting edge. If I could do more with hair, that would be my happy place."

"I'm excited for you then. I hope you discover what it is you want."

"You feel like helping me out then?"

"How so? Need someone to shampoo for you?" I asked, stepping back and rinsing out the suds.

"I was thinking you let me give you a new look."

I looked at the blue and purple locks and thought about what he was saying. It had been a few months since I'd changed it. "I could go for that. You always give me a killer look. What are you thinking?"

"I want to keep it a surprise."

Sighing, I fake rolled my eyes, knowing I trusted Simon to give me an awesome look. "Fine. But I want to tattoo something else on you then."

Simon took a deep breath but nodded. "Fair's fair."

We hurried through the rest of our shower and began to get ready, blow-drying and styling our hair. When we exited the bathroom, we found the brothers eating some food on the table. Slade pointed to a tray, and I eagerly walked over, my stomach ready for some delicious food. I was only in a robe, but I didn't rush to change since I was with all my boyfriends. Since Zane was here, Simon didn't feel the same and grabbed his bag, changing before joining us at the table.

"How was your workout?" I asked, looking at Slade and Zane.

"Not bad for a hotel gym," Zane said, smiling at me.

"I think you had your own workout," Slade rumbled, looking at me with heat in his eyes.

Taking a bite of a pancake, I shrugged, winking. I could tell he wanted to lunge for me and have his own way, but if we wanted to get to the farm when it opened so we had the most time to spend there, I knew I'd have to stop that train of thought.

"If we go and see the horses, we can pick one for me to take. Just think of all the rejected ones that don't fit the description. They need a home, too," I begged, puffing out my lip.

"Not happening."

"Fine." I pouted, sighing as I finished eating my pancake.

Getting up, I took a few slices of bacon with me as I dressed and finished packing our belongings. A few minutes later, we all headed to the van, excitement bubbling up in me at visiting the farm. Last night's altercation with the thief was a distant memory.

Sighing, I pushed it from my mind as I focused on the day ahead and what we would be preparing for tonight. Before I knew it, we were pulling into the gates of Grant's Farm. The place already had a magical quality, and the prospect of seeing animals had Zane and me bouncing in our seats.

"I'm so glad we made it here. This place houses over 900 rescue animals. It's the kind of thing I wouldn't mind doing someday," he said with a wistful voice. I peered over at Slade, and it seemed I wasn't the only one who had noticed his voice. I pinned it away, knowing I didn't want Zane to lose who he was. Being a vet was important to him, and I wanted to encourage that, however possible.

Since it had just opened, the line wasn't too long, and we were on the tram a few moments later, breezing through the grounds. The tour guide up front listed facts and pointed out the different types of animals. It felt like we were in the habitat with the animals and not in Missouri. This place was really cool.

Stepping off the tram and into the central part, I peered around, marveling at the architecture. "It's beautiful," I exclaimed, taking in all the different features.

"It was the Busch family home and designed using German architecture," Zane said, peering around.

"Ooh, goats!" I said, pointing to the booth where you could get a baby bottle to feed them. Zane and I ran over, grabbing a few as Simon and Slade watched. Zane showed me how to hold the bottle the best way to feed them, and we ran around the pen, trying to interact with as many goats as possible.

"This is amazing," I cried, overcome with emotion at how cute it was. When our bottles were empty, we headed out of the pen, and I jumped up and down, trying to tell Slade and Simon about it like they hadn't been standing there the whole time.

"Then this little brown one jumped on me, and the little gray one made a sound, and it was so cute. I take it back, Slade. I don't need a horse, just a baby goat!"

"Oh yes, goats are a reasonable thing to have as well," Zane chirped in, nodding at my idea.

"No," Slade said.

Rolling my eyes, I kept moving forward, looking at all the different animals. There were chickens, ducks, geese, peacocks, swans, llamas, and even parrots. But when I saw the lemur exhibit, I was in heaven.

"Oh, my God!" My hands flew to my mouth as I

began to bounce up and down. "Okay, I want a lemur. How cool would it be to walk around with it on my shoulder?"

Slade dropped his head, rubbing his temple. "Fuck. I'm going to have to buy her a goat just so she stops, aren't I?" he asked, the guys laughing at his plight.

Jumping on my toes, I wrapped my arms around his neck. "I love you, Tatzilla."

Slade's eyes bore into me, all sounds of the farm falling away as he held me at that moment in time. "I love you, Peach."

He kissed me, really kissed me, and I debated finding a spot to take that kiss further until Simon pulled us, reminding us we only had an hour left before we had to leave. The rest of the time, I walked hand in hand with Slade as we looked at all the animals. Simon and I even got to see where the Clydesdales were raised and bred. We stopped by the gift shop before we left, and I bought a tote bag and a pin, deciding I wanted to collect them from each place if I could.

As we stumbled back to the van, tiredness was setting in, and I was thankful I didn't have to drive. I felt a nap calling my name. Everyone was quiet as we began our journey to Branson, but it was a nice silence earned from fun-filled days and exhaustion.

"I think St. Louis is my favorite place. To Babs," I said as I drifted to sleep. The guys chuckled, but no one denied the magic the city had held or the amazing things we'd gotten to experience together, and I knew that Babs had been right. There was magic on the open road, and I was living it for once.

Chapter Eleven

THANE

WE'D BEEN DRIVING for a few hours, the soft snores of Simon and Lennox filling the space. I looked over at my brother, knowing this was my best chance to talk to him without him running away from the conversation.

"So, Dad asked if there was a day that worked best to meet up with him and Mia?" Watching him, I saw his hands grip the steering wheel before he sighed, turning to look at me.

"You're not going to let us get away with being too busy, are you?"

"Nope." I smiled, happy that I didn't have to walk around on eggshells with my brother. "It's time, Slade. Dad's changed, and I think it would be good for you two to bury the hatchet. He'll love Lennox."

He grunted, tapping his finger against the wheel. "Fine. But only a meal. I don't want to stay there."

"Fair enough," I said. Pulling out my phone, I sent a message stating we'd see him in a few days. He replied back instantly, saying he was looking forward to it. I turned toward the window, watching the world fly by as we cruised.

Slade cleared his throat, so I peeked over. He took the movement as an invitation to bring something up himself.

"I don't want you to feel like you have to give up being a vet. We can set something up at the house or see about getting you on with a vet in town if you want. I'm sure there are plenty of jobs."

"I appreciate that. The truth is, I don't know what I want to do anymore. I love being a vet, and I don't think it's something I want to quit altogether, but it also feels nice to not let it define me at the moment. I think I hid behind it, using it as an excuse to be unavailable. People respect veterinarians, especially when you do things like Vets without Borders. I didn't have to look too closely at myself and every-thing I was hiding. Meeting Lennox in person and facing everything that happened all those years ago opened me to new possibilities. I'm not ready to give up that freedom and perspective yet."

"Isn't that scary, though? Not knowing what

you're going to do? You were always the one with the plan."

"Yeah, it is." I looked at him, seeing the brother who'd been my best friend when we were kids. The one I had before our parents' divorce, and we became divided. "But I'm not scared. It's kind of exciting in a way to get to figure out what else I might be good at. It's a privilege not many people get or often take, so I'm not going to waste it."

"You always were the optimistic one. It's good to see that light shining bright in you again. I…" he stopped, clearing his throat. "I hadn't realized how much I missed having you around. I'm glad you're here, man. For what it's worth, I selfishly hope you take a while to figure out what you want so I can spend more time with you."

"Ah, bro, that's the sweetest thing you've ever said to me," I teased, knowing he needed some reprieve from the mushy stuff.

He peered back, seeing that they were still asleep. "Yeah, well, Peach has taught me to share my feelings and not hide them. I love what I do and get to do it with her. I can admit I have it made. I just want you to find your thing too."

"Me too." I reached over and squeezed his bicep, letting him know I appreciated his vulnerability. "Speaking of. I got your Instagram account changed over to the new shop name. I'll post new content once we get to the convention. I'm excited to see you both in action."

"Yeah, hopefully, it won't be hell. I like to work in my studio without an audience," he grunted.

"It will be a good learning experience for you then. Sometimes I think you take the tortured artist thing to the extreme."

He laughed, his whole body shaking. "Okay, you might be right. There was a time when it was true, but I can't say I'm tortured anymore. Peach makes me happy. Simon makes me happy. Having you back makes me happy."

"I never imagined us having to share a girlfriend, but I can't deny I'm good with how it turned out. It's nice getting to share life with you again."

"Okay, we're verging on too much emotion. We need to change the topic." Slade chuckled, switching lanes with ease as he maneuvered around the traffic.

"Ah, but I like listening to you talk," a small voice said from the back, and I turned, finding Lennox staring at us.

"Hey, Noxy girl, how are you?"

"I feel more rested." She moved to sit up, making Simon grumble as he was shifted around. She stretched her arms, her boobs moving with the motion, and I found myself staring. "How long did I sleep for?" she asked.

"A few hours. We have about an hour left."

She nodded, reached into the cooler, and pulled out a drink and a snack. "You guys want anything?"

"Sure."

She handed a drink to Slade and me before sitting back in her seat, watching the mountains as she hummed along to the radio. Listening to her sing, I knew she needed to pursue it. She loved music, and it was only stage fright keeping her from doing it.

"You know," I whispered, "if you were to play with her, I bet she'd be more inclined to sing."

I watched my brother from the corner of my eye, noticing his jaw tense. His eyes flicked to Lennox, a rare smile graced his face as he watched her. He could deny it all he wanted, but he knew I was right.

"She needs to sing. The world should hear her. You two together would be diabolical."

"Big words," he said, sniffing as he merged with traffic for the exit.

"Yeah, but you can't deny I'm right. Just… think about it. I think she would go along more if she didn't do it alone. You loved playing the guitar. I think it would be good for you to reconnect with that part of yourself, too."

As we pulled onto Route 76, Lennox gasped, and

I heard her shifting as she woke up Simon. "Look! Good gravy! It's like Gatlinburg. Oh! There's Dolly Parton's Stampede!" She kept calling out places as we crawled along in the traffic.

Lennox wasn't wrong, just like the famous city in Tennessee, Branson was known for its theaters and entertainment.

"I think there are over fifty theaters in Branson alone," I found myself saying.

"Really? That's cool."

"What time do we have to register?" I asked, looking at Simon.

"We have an hour before the doors will open and then they will give us the information," he read, looking at his phone. "We need to check in at the hotel with the coordinator. They should all be close together."

We pulled up to Branson Landing, finding the hotel with a boardwalk waterfront. The convention center was next door, making it a convenient location to host this. Quicker than last time, we unloaded our belongings, checked in, and made our way to our suite. Again, Slade had upgraded, giving us more room to spread out. I figured it was so we had two rooms in case anyone needed alone time, which was mostly for me I figured, and I appreciated the gesture.

There were times I knew I needed Lennox to myself and times when I didn't mind joining them, but I also understood there were moments they required as a threesome to connect without me too. So far, we hadn't had any difficulty figuring it out, and I hoped it remained that way.

"Let's freshen up, and then we need to find the coordinator and get our registration packets. There shouldn't be too much after that to do."

"Sounds like a plan!" Lennox chirped, jumping on the bed.

"Peach, get down, or I'll have to tackle you."

"Oh?" she teased, still bouncing. Slade didn't waste any time tackling her to the bed, both of them laughing as they bounced.

Taking our bags over to the dresser, I helped Simon sort out items and place them in as much order as we could have in a hotel room with four people.

"Lenn, you need to change?"

She looked down, taking in her strawberry dress. "Nah. I'm good. Let's roll."

Together, we made it down to the ballroom where tables were set up and separated by profession and last name. Simon headed off to the stylish side of the room, and I followed Slade and Lennox. I'd already gotten the message from Slade to go with Lenn, so she wasn't standing in line alone.

"Name and shop?" a bored worker asked, not even looking up.

"James and Tattooed Hearts." That had the person looking up, and I wondered what for.

"You're Lennox James?" she asked, and I felt the hair on my neck raise at the question.

"Yeah," Lennox said, peering at me, her face as confused as mine. "Why?"

At her confirmation, the worker's face changed, and she smiled widely, making me relax slightly.

"I'm a huge fan. I follow you on Insta and LiveIt. I was so excited when I saw you were going to be here. I even bribed my friend to switch tables. I was beginning to think you weren't going to show. Can I be one of the people you tattoo?" she asked, her words tumbling out at top speed.

"Um, hi. I guess. I'm not sure how that works." Again, Lennox looked at me, anxiety beginning to build that she might disappoint someone.

"In case she doesn't get to pick, how about a selfie for now?" I suggested, hoping to ease some of her anxiety.

"Oh yes! That would be amazing. Here, let me come out." Quicker than I'd thought possible, the girl was around the table, shoving her phone in my face and preening next to Lennox.

"Cheese," they both said as I snapped a few photos, trying not to laugh at the whole situation. I handed the phone back, and the girl hugged Lennox quickly before walking back to her spot and beginning to review the information packet.

"Here's your booth number. You'll be next to the other member from your shop. You have two hours to set up tonight and will be expected to be at your booth tomorrow thirty minutes before the doors open. The first two hours will consist of showcasing your shop and for guests to look around at all the booths. There will be signup forms at your table for people to fill out. You don't have to take the first person as your subject. You're able to look at what they want and decide. You're under no obligation, but it gives you a list of people interested in your work to start with and find the perfect client for the competition. Once you have that finalized, there will be forms for them to sign. That will start at 1 pm. Until then, you can practice by giving smaller tattoos or just talking to people, looking around, or sketching. Each artist has their own ritual. After the hair portion of the contest, you'll be given an hour for lunch, and then you'll be on the clock. It's not about being the fastest, but that is a component. You'll be graded on skill, artistry, and time. Each convention will crown one winner, who will be invited back for the grand finale showcase at the end of the summer. You only have to win once to be eligible. You'll also be given a ranking that you will carry from city to city, depending on how many you choose to do. At the end of the season, you could be eligible to win the grand prize regardless if you make it to the showcase."

She took a deep breath, smiling at Lennox like she hung the moon.

"Any questions? I can give you my number in case you have some later and need to ask. That wouldn't be a problem at all."

Chuckling, I took the packet of papers and showed Lennox where to sign for the liability waiver and that she was to accept no compensation for the tattoos performed during the competition. Once she had the paperwork done, I placed the lanyard over her head, enjoying getting to touch her. It was a hard job, but someone had to do it.

"I do have one question… I'm sorry, what was your name, hun?" Lennox asked, her accent thick.

"It's Esther."

"Hi, Esther. Could my boyfriend get an assistant badge? Would that be possible?"

"Oh, I'm not supposed to, but I'll make an exception for you." She winked as she leaned over and grabbed a badge from a box under the table. "Just promise me you won't misuse your power," she said, holding onto the lanyard like it was a golden ticket.

"I promise."

"Thank you so much, Esther. It was great meeting you, and you should totally sign up. You never know."

"Oh, I will. Bye." She waved enthusiastically as we left, finding Simon and Slade waiting for us at the door.

"What was that all about?" Slade asked as I shook my head, chuckling.

"Just someone else falling in love with our girl."

"Too bad," he growled, pulling her under his arm, looking over his shoulder like someone was going to come and steal her right from under his nose.

"Oh nice, you got a badge," Simon said, noticing the lanyard.

"Yeah, Lennox used her charm to get it for me. I hadn't thought of that. It would've sucked to not be able to be with y'all."

"I was wondering if you could help me while I'm competing, actually?" Simon asked hesitantly. "If it's not too much trouble."

"Absolutely. Just put me to work."

"Awesome. I think this is going to be amazing. Thanks for supporting me when I suggested it."

We'd dropped back behind Slade and Lennox and I looked over at him. "Of course. I know we're not brothers like Slade and me, but I consider you one. I'm glad we're able to bond more as well."

I bumped his shoulder, some of his anxiety leaving him as he smiled at me. "Good, me too, and I'm glad."

We headed to the convention center, and I looked around at everything. I never pictured myself here, but I couldn't deny that it fit in a weird way. I think it was time for me to step out from behind my shield and see what else life had to offer me.

I MOVED a pot of ink around for the millionth time, positioning everything on my stand just so. We had a booth with our shop name and portfolios on display. Zane had even managed to print some things off at the hotel last night, so we had signs with our social media handles, the location of the shop, and the website. It was wise to direct people to where they could find out more information.

"It's good, Peach," Slade said, coming up to me and pulling me back against his chest.

"I've just never done something with an audience before."

"Sure you have. You just didn't know it. I was always watching."

"You know, that could be taken as creepy. Good thing I like your weirdness."

"Humph," he grunted, his tattooed knuckles splaying across my belly, contrasting with the rose and skull dress I was wearing. "Just go to your happy place. Don't worry about anyone else. Focus on your client and you'll be fine. You got your music?"

I nodded, my shoulders relaxing. "You going to be okay?" I asked, looking up at him.

"Yeah. I'll be fine. I don't really care about this competition. Only enough to stay in it so we can stay together. I think Simon needs it, so I'll do it for him."

I spun around, his hands transferring from my belly to my bum, and I lifted up, wrapping my arms around his neck. "It's sexy how much you love him, you know?"

"Oh?" he asked, his eyes shining back with love.

"Yeah." I licked my lips, shifting on my feet when Simon and Zane returned, dropping off their things at the booth.

"Hey, how's your station?" I asked, dropping my arms and trying to quell the lust. The redness in my cheeks gave away my intentions if Simon's smirk was anything to go by.

"It'll do. It's weird not having a lot of space. Since I'm not here with a salon, I'm shoved at the end."

"That sucks—" A loud alarm sounded, cutting me off.

"Attention. Doors will be opening in fifteen minutes. Please make sure you're at your stations now. Good Luck!"

"I guess that means it's time to leave again." Simon hung his head, and I hated that he had to be alone.

"Zane, will you hang out with Si?"

"Already planning on it, Noxy girl." He dipped down, giving me a kiss on the cheek. "Good luck. Kick some ass."

"Thanks."

Simon pulled me away, hugging me. "Always looking out for me. Come visit when you can, okay?"

"I'll be your biggest fan."

Smiling, he stepped back and kissed me quickly before walking over to Slade. I fixed my dress, smoothed the fabric, and ran my fingers through my hair. The first two hours were schmoozing, and then we had a break while the hair stylists competed.

I could do this. *I could do this.*

Voices began to trickle through, and I assumed the doors were open. Slade pulled me down to my chair, placing his arm along the back. He was staking his claim. I didn't think he had anything to worry about, though.

When people started to swarm our table a few minutes later, we both stood there in shock as they asked us questions, talking about some of our work they'd seen on social media.

"Lennox, I loved that one you did with the flowers and books. It was beautiful," a girl said, smiling at me.

"Oh, thank you," I replied, finding myself blushing.

"What kind of tattoos would you give me?" someone asked Slade. He stared at them, not answering.

"A tattoo is personal. It should mean something to you," I said, leaning closer to my tatzilla.

"Good point," the kid said, his cheeks reddening.

Slade's hand dropped down to my waist, making it even more apparent we were together. Laughing, I shook my head, talking to the people as they asked us questions. We had a few people sign up and put what they wanted tattooed. Esther made sure to walk by and add her name to the list. I looked at what she wanted and showed it to Slade, who shrugged, not making any comment. The time went by fast, and we had twenty people to choose from by the end.

"How do we even pick someone?" I asked, looking at the list.

"First, we mark off the people who only want a free tattoo." He took a sharpie and marked off five people. "Then we mark off the people with unrealistic expectations for this competition." Slade marked off another eight, and I had to admit he was right. Some of the tattoos would take all day, and this was only a three-hour competition. "Next to go are boring people who have no imagination." He marked off another four people, leaving three people on the list —Esther included.

"Wow, okay. That makes it easier." Covering up the names, I looked at the three things there, seeing if any of them sparked creativity in me.

A LION AND SKULL COMBO.

Sunflowers entwined with music notes.

A heart with multiple swords stuck in it.

"YOU KNOW you want the sunflower one, Peach. Just do it." Slade nudged me, and I looked up, meeting his eyes. Grinning, I nodded, feeling happy. My fingers were already itching to start sketching.

"Which are you going to do?"

Slade closed his eyes and pointed to one. Looking at the paper, I laughed when I saw it was the lion and skull one.

"Can you message them? I want to go check on Simon."

"Fine." He pulled out his phone and typed in the numbers, sending them quick messages. Knowing him, it was probably something like, "You. 1 pm. Tattooed Hearts."

Chuckling to myself, I walked around the booths, looking at some of the other tattoo artists as I made my way over. I'd been too nervous to look at other people's setups, but I knew I'd have to peruse their portfolios sometime later. From what I could see, there were some talented people here. When I got to the hair section, it took me a while to find Simon. He was far away from all the others like he was an afterthought. I could see him and Zane standing, but it didn't look like they had anyone stopping and talking to them.

"Hey," I said as I neared. "We picked our people, so I have a little break. How's it going?"

Simon looked at all the other booths. "I'm like the beauty school dropout. I didn't think this through, Lenn. No one has signed up."

"What? That's insane. You're crazy talented."

"Yeah, but with no salon to back me, it's like I'm invisible." He slumped back into his chair, looking dejected.

"What if you do my hair now?" I asked. "Weren't you wanting to practice? Well, here's your opportunity."

He sat up, looking hopeful. "Would that work, though? When do you compete?"

"We don't start until after lunch. So, I have time. I can work on the sketch while you have me in your chair."

"Are you sure, Lenn?" He leaned forward like he was too excited to believe it. I didn't know why he thought I'd say no. I never could.

"Si, it's perfect. I get a new look, and you get to show all these snobs how amazing you are."

He beamed, practically bouncing out of his seat as he jumped. He lifted me into his arms, swinging me around as he hugged me.

"I love you, Lemon Drop." He kissed my cheek, setting me back on the ground as he rushed off to the coordinators. A few other hairstylists looked at us curiously, but no one moved to talk to us.

"Geez. I never knew hairstylists were so stuck up," I whispered to Zane.

"Yeah, Simon told me about some of the troubles he's faced being a bisexual stylist in the south and how it's very elitist. If you don't work for one of the big salons, then you're not worth it."

"That's dumb," I huffed, crossing my arms.

Simon returned a few minutes later, and I sent Zane to get my sketchbook from Slade and fill him in on what was happening. Simon had me in his chair, lifting my hair muttering, as he jotted some things into a notebook on what he wanted to do.

"Anything?" he asked, and I nodded, trusting Simon.

"Who do I need to punch?" Slade asked a few minutes later, my sketchbook in his hand. He glared at the people closest to us, making his dissatisfaction known.

"No one. It's fine. Lennox saved the day." Simon lifted my hair and let it fall, ignoring the thunderous man in front of him.

"It's better this way, Tatzilla. I get a new look and Simon will get noticed. Now, can I have my book before you break it?"

His eyes dropped to mine, and he took a deep breath before handing me my stuff. "Thane's going to man the booth. I'm going to watch you two."

Rolling my eyes, I knew nothing we said would deter him. He felt he had to protect us, and I would never tell him how hot I thought it was. He already had a big enough ego.

The announcer came over, briefly going over the rules and what a person was rated on. Like the tattoos, it was based more on style, skill, and overall effect versus time. When she dropped her hand and yelled "go," it was like a frenzy.

Simon whirled me around, his scissors already in

his hand, and trimmed a few spots before beginning to mix the color he wanted. While he did that, I started to draw in my book. The sunflowers were different to draw, and I enjoyed the challenge. I began to add some music notes to the petals and in the dead space around them. I had a couple of different varieties to show Esther when I was done, feeling happy with the finished product.

I looked up and found Slade smiling at me. I'd gotten lost in my drawing, letting Simon move me as he needed. I turned and saw him checking the foils where he'd separated my hair. "It's ready to rinse," he said, his voice serious. Simon's work voice was always something that got my engine going for some strange reason.

He helped me walk over to the shampoo station and pulled the foils out, rinsing my hair thoroughly. I zoned out as he washed it, enjoying the head massage. Simon got to work as soon as my butt hit the chair, adding framing layers around my face. I found Slade looking through my sketchbook.

"What do you think?"

"It's good. You should win." He closed it, keeping it close. I wasn't worried about competing with him. We didn't need to with one another.

When Simon began to blow dry my hair, I blinked, not realizing he was done. He worked so efficiently when he was in the zone. There wasn't a mirror, so I couldn't see what it looked like. Slade kept staring, though, which made me curious.

When Simon turned me around, I wasn't sure what to expect. I blinked a few times, not believing it was me.

"Wow, Si. I love it." I swished the pink and green locks back and forth, loving how it moved.

"It's what I call *Watermelon Sugar*," he said, blushing.

"It's amazing." I preened up at him, loving how much he brought my hair to life so effortlessly.

"I just need to take a picture," the official from SIT said, standing in front of Simon's booth. She looked impressed, making me hope that Simon would be taken seriously now.

"Okay, you're good to go. We'll announce the winners after the tattoo competition."

The guys and I returned to the booth, finding that Zane had gotten us some food. Esther came by, selecting her design, and I got it ready on the transfer paper while we ate.

"Alright, ladies and gents, it's time for our tattoo round."

At the sound of go, tattoo guns began to buzz, filling the space. "I'm going to listen to music. But let me know if you're not okay."

Esther nodded, leaning back. I was putting the sunflowers on her upper thigh. It was between the size of my palm and hand. It would be close to the three-hour mark with the coloring and shading I'd added.

The music covered the noise, and I fell into my happy place as I began to outline the sunflowers. It was only when my hand started to cramp, and my neck ached that I realized how focused I'd been. I glanced up, finding that Esther was reading a book. The cover looked cool, and I made a mental note to ask her who the author was. I could always use a new book to read.

Stretching my fingers and rotating my neck, I zeroed in on my design, happy with how it'd turned out. When I finished it, I sat back, the satisfaction of a job well done filling me. I pulled out my earbuds and found Esther beaming at me.

"Oh, wow! I love it."

"We need to catalog it," a SIT official said, and I glanced up, seeing that most people were done and had been watching me. A few people clapped, talking about it. I looked over at Slade's station, finding his eyes on me. He smiled, nodding. His way of telling me I'd done well.

Cleaning up, I went over the aftercare and explained what she would need to do to keep the colors vibrant. By the time everything was put away, it was already time for them to announce the winners.

"For best hair color, the award goes to Simon Fisher."

Simon stood, shocked, and I had to nudge him to go and accept his award. I noticed many people were looking at him differently after that too. Take that, snobs.

"For the best tattoo design, the award goes to Lennox James, from Tattooed Hearts in Bowling Green, Kentucky." This time it was Simon and Zane who had to nudge me to walk up there.

"For the fastest tattoo, the award goes to Slade Evans, also from Tattooed Hearts in Bowling Green, Kentucky."

Slade walked up, taking his award, not smiling the whole time. After a few more awards, with first-place overall going to someone from Inkjection studio, we went back to our booth to pack up.

"Not bad for our first one," I said, zipping the last of our ink into the bag.

"It wasn't as horrible as I imagined," Slade muttered, winking at me. "I enjoyed the view, at least."

"Do you know what places you want to visit tomorrow? I was thinking for tonight, we'd grab some food and then just hit the pool or relax in the room," Zane offered, picking up a tote of things.

"Yeah, that sounds good to me. I'm peopled out."

"Nice job," a man I didn't know said, stepping up to our booth. Slade ignored him, throwing one of the bags over his arm.

"Ah, just going to ignore me then," the man said, chuckling at Slade. His eyes turned to me, and I didn't like how they fell over my body. "Now you, my lovely dear, were amazing. Some of the shading you did was perfection. Why are you wasting your talent in some backwater tattoo shop? You should be in the big city. Here's my card if you ever get adventurous."

"Bless your heart," I cooed. "Aren't you just precious? I guess you've never had to deal with a rutting chicken before if you think our backwater town isn't exciting."

Grabbing Slade's hand, I pulled him away, leaving the man gaping after us. As soon as we were clear, Simon and Zane burst out laughing, needing to stop at one point to gather themselves.

"What's a rutting chicken?" Zane asked me, wiping his eyes.

"No clue. But it sounded like something a hick might say, and since he thought we were beneath him, I went with it. He'll be too scared to look it up."

I shrugged, making Slade breakout into laughter this time.

"Oh, Peach, I love you. That was Lee from Inkjection. We interned at the same parlor, and he's hated me ever since. He's a tool."

"Then I guess we better work on our game to take them down."

"I love your ruthlessness, Peach." Slade kissed me, pulling me along to the room. "And now I'm ravenous."

The look in his eyes told me it wasn't just for food either.

Chapter Thirteen

LOOKING AT PEACH, I could only think about getting her naked, her creamy skin on display for me to devour. Her new hair color stood out bright against the landscape, pulling everyone's eyes to her. It was enough to make me want to claim her right in front of everyone so they'd back the fuck off.

A growl escaped me, echoing my thoughts and I grabbed her hand, pulling her through the crowd, unable to take their stares. I loved that people finally noticed her and gave my girl the credit she was due. But I didn't like the calculating looks or the gleam of what they could take or use her for. Lennox was more than a hot commodity. She was generous, sweet, and passionate, and I'd never let anyone take advantage of that.

Things calmed some when we exited the convention center and the crowd dispersed. Branson was lit up along the strip, calling us to come and investigate what lay behind the doors. If I hadn't been exhausted from the day, it would've been fun to do some things with our group. But my brother had the right idea about escaping to the room. It sounded like the best place to be at the moment.

Thankfully, the hotel wasn't too far. I stopped in my tracks and began looking around at what food options were close. When I spotted a food truck, I didn't even care what they served as I made my way there, dragging Peach with me. The smell hit us as we neared, my stomach growling on command.

"Oh, this smells amazing," Peach cooed, inhaling the food deeply.

"Yeah, good choice, man," my brother said, slapping me on the back.

Simon snorted, shaking his head as Lennox and Thane began to look at the menu. He stopped next to me, smiling. "You just stopped at the first place you saw, didn't you?"

"Humph," I grunted, casting my eyes over to him. "You'll never know." Smiling at teasing him, I relished the feeling of being so open with both him and Lennox now. It felt like my life was finally moving in the direction it was always meant to go.

After ordering copious amounts of food, we

carried it to our room. We dug into the pulled pork, loaded fries, and apple cobbler, none of us speaking as we ate in a trance. I looked around the table when it was cleared, taking in everyone's state.

"What's it going to be? Swimming or movie?"

The three of them thought about it, but in the end, we all decided a dip in the pool sounded nice. While they all changed, I called down to the front desk with a mission.

"Hello, Mr. Evans. How can I help you?"

"How much for me to secure the pool for two hours?"

"I'm not sure I understand, sir."

"Oh, you understand. How much will it cost me to ensure no one else can access the pool? The *topside* pool."

"Well, um, sir, I'm not sure."

"Listen, you might think I want this for nefarious reasons, but that's not the case. My girlfriend is famous, and we'd like to be able to enjoy the pool without people taking photos or asking for things. I know that you do this for other celebs. So, call your manager and get back to me."

I hung up, rolling my eyes at the man's incompetence. A giggle had me jerking my head up to find Peach staring at me.

"I'm famous, am I?" She wiggled her eyebrows.

I couldn't focus on anything else as I locked on her swimsuit. It wasn't that it was skimpy. Peach had more bits covered than most swimsuits, but it wrapped around her body just right, making me want to unwrap the beautiful package she was, especially with just a hint of her tattoo showing. Swallowing, I looked back up, finding her cheeks red. I started to say something when the phone rang.

"Do you have an answer?" I asked in lieu of a hello.

"Um, yes, he said $500." I heard the man on the line gulp as he repeated it, probably expecting me to be outraged at the price. Honestly, I'd been willing to pay anything to spend time with Peach without interruption. I had more money than I needed, and if it got me memories and time with the people I loved, then it was well spent.

"Deal."

"Oh, okay, um, someone will be up with the key card and for you to sign off. There's apparently a liability waiver, etc."

"Fine, but don't take too long." I hung up, not waiting for another answer.

"What did you do now?" Simon asked, walking out with a towel draped over his shoulder. His shorts hung low on his hips, showing off the V I loved so much. He didn't have muscles like Thane or me, but Simon was delicious in his own right.

Smirking, he walked closer, snapping his fingers in front of my face. "Babe, focus. What did you do?" he asked, just as a knock sounded.

This time it was my turn to smirk as I didn't answer, walking over to the door. I opened it, finding two people. They both tried to peer around me to see into the room, probably to figure out who the famous person was. Blocking their view with my body, I held out my hand for the forms.

"We just need you to sign here," one of the hotel workers said, handing me a clipboard. Skimming it, I took in the information and signed off. It wouldn't be needed. I'd keep everyone safe.

Once I handed it back, they gave me a black leather case that had the slip for the charge. I signed it quickly, handing it back. Once they had both things, they handed me the key.

"After the two hours, it will be deactivated."

Nodding, I took the key and stepped back to close the door. One of the more ambitious ones stepped forward, trying to stop the door.

"Could we get a picture?"

"No." I didn't wait, shutting the door and locking it. I waited for them to leave, watching through the peephole. Once it was clear, I turned back to the room, checking everyone over. Peach now had a soft dress covering most of her body, making my heart slow at knowing people wouldn't get a peek at what she had under it. Thane and Simon both had shirts and towels in their hands.

"Ready?" I asked, and they all nodded, and we left the hotel room and headed toward the stairs. Since we were on the top floor, the private pool was only accessible from the stairwell. Swiping the keycard, it lit up green, giving us entrance.

"Wow," Lennox said as she stepped onto the roof. "This is amazing. How did you know?" She spun around, taking in all the lights. From this height, you could see the whole boulevard with all the theaters as their signs lit up the night.

"Traveling secret," Thane said, winking. "There are a lot of perks nice hotels have if you know how to ask for them."

"Since this is my second time in a hotel, I'm very impressed. I'm not counting staying in the motel because it was gross." She did a full-body convulsion, making us laugh, but a small ounce of shame wafted through me at knowing why she had been in one—me.

She walked over and leaned against the wall as she looked out at the city. It wasn't until then that I realized how new of an experience this was for her, making me vow to do more things like this. Peach deserved it all.

"Well, we have two hours, so we better use it. Set a timer. The last thing we want is to be locked out."

Before Peach had time to think about it, I picked her up and jumped into the pool. She shrieked and giggled the whole way, letting me know she wouldn't be too mad at me. The pool water was warm as we splashed, the water rushing to welcome us into its embrace. I kept my arms around her, not letting her go as we sank to the bottom. Kicking up, I quickly had us emerging, the water rolling off our faces.

"I'm so going to get you for that," she said, slapping my arm.

"Oh? What are you going to do about it, Peach?" I lifted my eyebrow in a challenge. She wrapped her legs around me, giving me a coy smile.

"I'll wait until you least expect it. Then I'll strike. Now, swim over to the side so I can take this off. It's heavy wet."

"Yes, ma'am."

Swimming over to the edge, she pulled off her dress and tossed it onto the poolside, the slopping sound as it landed echoing around us. Simon walked over and picked it up, wringing it out before laying it on a chair to dry.

"Watch this, Noxy girl," Thane bellowed before he cannon-balled right next to us. Laughing, we splashed him as he emerged, resulting in an epic water fight.

After a while, we all just floated together, enjoying the peacefulness of the night without anyone else around.

When I felt like everyone had decompressed enough from the day, I swam over to Peach and began to kiss her neck. She sucked in a breath, turning to look at me. Simon saw what I was doing and swam closer, closing her in from the front.

The water made her skin slick as I ran my hands over her. Her legs wrapped around Simon, so I took it upon myself to unwrap the present I'd been dying for. Once I had her top off, I laid her back in the water and began to nibble on her tits. They bobbed perfectly in the water, her nipples peeking out of it.

"Can I join?" Thane asked, swimming up to the other side.

"Yes," Lennox breathed in response, but it was me he was waiting for. Nodding, I focused on the task at hand, filling my hands with her gorgeous mounds as I kissed and licked her all over.

"Should we move out of the water, so we don't drown?"

"That's part of the fun." Thane made an irritated

sound, so I rolled my eyes, looking up. "Fine. We can move to the steps."

The pool had an excellent swim-up section that was only about two feet deep, with steps half in the water and out. Positioning Peach, she sat on the floor, leaving her upper body out of the water. An idea came to me, and I pulled my throbbing dick out of my swim shorts. Sitting down, I pulled Lennox over to me. She easily fell into my chest, letting me direct her where to go. Sliding her down my length, we both moaned as the water worked as a natural lubricant.

"Fuck, that's hot," Simon groaned, watching us. He moved over to the side where he could kiss us both as Thane stayed on the other, taking over my job on her breasts. When his hand began to snake down lower, I broke my kiss and growled out a warning for him.

"I know, I know. Don't touch your dick."

When I was getting closer, I took over, directing Peach up and down my cock in the motion I needed, feeling my balls draw up as the blood rushed to my cock. Thrusting up one last time, I came in her so hard, that I saw stars for a few seconds.

Thane took over, pulling Lennox to his front as I focused on Simon, who was stroking his dick, licking his lips. He leaned back on the steps, giving me the perfect height to lick him. Taking his cock into my mouth, I pulled his ass closer as I swallowed him. I could hear Thane and Lennox fucking next to me, and it spurred me on, a silent competition to see who could make their partner cum first.

Tightening my grip, I twisted and sucked him up and down, not stopping even when he hit the back of my throat, my eyes watering. Loosening my throat, I managed to take him a little further as I massaged his balls, moving my thumb to his backdoor. When I could feel his legs tensing, I pressed my thumb in, and I felt his back arch as he came with a shout erupting down my throat.

Pulling back, I licked every last drop as I took in my boyfriend with a pleased smile.

"You shouldn't be allowed to look this good and be that amazing at that. It's not fair to the rest of the population," he panted, trying to catch his breath.

"Good thing I don't care about the rest of the world."

"Oh, that's right. You're an asshole. It negates everything else." He laughed, winking at me.

"I think Peach prefers alpha-hole."

I turned, finding Thane kneeling as he lifted Lennox up and down, and I could tell they were close. Almost like he could hear my thoughts, they both fell apart. Lennox fell into him, her moan long and languid. When a weird cricket sound started, I looked around, wondering what it was.

"It's the alarm. I set it to go off 15 minutes before we needed to leave. I guess it's time to get out."

"Best. Pool. Party. Ever," Peach said, smiling widely.

We all climbed out and dried off, getting redressed if needed. As we gathered our things, I looked out into the city, knowing it would forever hold a special meaning to me now.

Chapter Fourteen

LENNOX

THE MUSIC GROUP on stage finished their last number, and I clapped along with the crowd, rising to give them a standing ovation. Something in me had come alive watching them perform, and I wasn't quite sure what it was.

Actually, if I thought about it, things started to change in me the moment we'd set out on our adventure. And now, this need in me was beginning to burn like an inferno, no longer willing to be caged.

"What did you think, Peach?" Slade asked, draping his arm around me. Beaming up at him, I couldn't help but let my face do the talking.

"It was amazing. I was kind of jealous, actually."

As he began to steer me toward the exit, his eyebrow arched up in question. Simon and Zane followed behind us, their excitement occasionally reaching us as they talked about the show.

Today had been filled with a lot of new experiences. We'd started it off with waffles and pancakes at one of the many pancake houses, then did an ATV tour of the Ozark Mountains. I'd decided that being in the mountains was becoming one of my favorite places to be. I'd once thought the hills and valleys of Kentucky were my favorite, but even Kentucky bluegrass couldn't compete with the mountains.

After the tour, we went to the Titanic museum and the World's largest toy museum. We'd had a quick rest before we hit the dinner show. It had been a full day, but I'd loved every second of it.

"You tired, Peach?" Slade asked once we made it out onto the street.

"No, I'm kind of wired. I don't know what it was about their show, but I feel like I have all this energy coursing through me."

"We should check out the karaoke bar Esther suggested," Simon offered, giving me a look. In fact, all three guys were looking at me, waiting for my answer.

"That sounds perfect, actually." They all beamed at me, relaxing, and I wasn't sure what they were so tense about.

"I think it's close by," Zane stated, already on his phone. "Follow me."

Simon grabbed my hand as Slade moved up next to his brother, and we made our four-person caravan for the trip to the bar. Walking into the place, I was instantly in love. It was filled with bright lights, neon of every color, and looked like a throwback to the '80s. The walls were lined with pinball machines and soft couches, while giant bean bags were in the center in lieu of chairs.

"Okay, this is my new favorite bar."

There was a stage up front where a girl was singing a bad rendition of a Britney Spears song.

"I'll hit her to stop," Zane mumbled, making us all laugh.

"Violence is never the answer," I stated, knowing he'd been making a play off the lyric and not actually intending to hit her, but I didn't want to condone it either way.

"You're right. That was in bad taste. I'll pay her to stop?" he asked.

"Better." Giggling, I pulled him close and kissed him, letting him know I wasn't upset. When he pulled back, his eyes were hooded, a smirk filling his face.

"I changed my mind. Karaoke is a horrible idea," he said, making me laugh.

"Nope. If I'm here, then we're all doing it." We walked over to a table that had just been cleared, sitting on the soft cushions. There was a QR code on the hardwood surface, so I pulled out my phone and scanned it. It brought up the bar's app, where we could place drink and food orders, and put in our karaoke songs.

"Genius!" I exclaimed, already submitting a few drink and food orders. The guys laughed at me, but my biggest pet peeve was never getting service. The guys were hot; so, they didn't understand that a girl my size and with a quirky sense of style was often overlooked when it came to fast service.

Scrolling through the songs, I leaned over to Slade, who was talking with Simon on his other side and pointed to one. He lifted his eyebrow in question, waiting for me to spell it out.

"Sing with me? I'm sure there's a guitar you could borrow."

Slade stared into my eyes for a long while, and I was about to tell him to forget it when he let out a breath and nodded. I knew he hated being the center of attention as much as I did, so maybe if we did it together, it wouldn't be as bad. Kissing his cheek, I entered my information just as a round of drinks were set down on the table.

"Welcome to Throwback. Anything else I can get

you at the moment?" the waiter asked, looking us all over.

"We're good," Zane replied, having the best manners apparently. Once the waiter was gone, I looked around the room, taking everything in.

"This kind of reminds me of the night we met," Zane said, leaning closer to me.

"Yeah, it kind of does." I knocked into his shoulder, smiling as I took a sip of my drink. The tartness exploded across my tongue, quickly followed by the sweet, balancing it out. "Oh, yum. This is great." I sucked it down more, the rush going to my head a little.

"Slow down, Peach. I want to understand your lyrics, not your slurs."

"It's non-alcoholic," I said, sticking my tongue out at him. "The worst I'll get is a sugar high."

Slade stared me down, not backing away from his statement, and I rolled my eyes. Sometimes, he was such a spoilsport. Thankfully, our food arrived soon after, distracting us all.

"I know we just ate, but that felt like hours ago," Simon said as he popped a pretzel dog into his mouth.

"This doesn't count as food. It's like after-dinner snacks," I said, taking a bite of the cheesecake ball.

The guys snorted at my assessment as my phone

buzzed, making me jump. Looking down, I saw a notification from the app stating that it was time to head to the stage.

"Oh! It's us. We're up!" I took one more bite and followed it with a drink before standing and pulling Slade with me. He didn't make it easy, but eventually followed me to the side of the stage.

"Name?" the tech asked, standing to the side with a tablet in their hand.

"Lennox. And do you have a guitar?" I asked.

"Yeah, it should be tuned." He nodded to a section where different instruments were, and Slade walked over, picking up a few guitars before finding one he liked. He pulled the strap over his head and began to pick a few chords, testing it himself.

"You're up," the tech said, drawing my attention back to the stage.

Slade followed, sitting on a stool while I took the microphone. The lights shined down on us, making me a little blind to the crowd, which always helped me focus on the music. Nerves began to fill me, but I shook them away, reminding myself no one knew me here and it was just for fun.

Slade began to play the opening chords, slapping his hand on the guitar between beats as the rest of the music track began to play behind us. Looking at him, I started singing the lyrics to "Ho Hey" by the Lumineers. It was a favorite of mine, and I was glad he was willing to sing it with me.

When the chorus came, he joined in, our voices melding together in perfect harmony. I smiled, feeling more at ease the longer we sang. The next verse came, and he took it, changing one of the words, making me laugh.

"I think you're right for me. Look at what we've been." His eyes pierced me as he sang, filling my heart even more.

When the chorus came around again, I joined in, feeling as if we could do anything, the adrenaline of singing together, pumping through me. That notion from earlier of coming alive felt even stronger, and I wondered what it all meant.

Singing the last verse, we ended the song, staring at one another. I jumped when the applause broke out, having forgotten the audience was even there. Turning back to the microphone, I smiled, waving as we headed off the stage. The tech guy stared at us, giving us a respectful nod as we returned to our table. A couple of people called out to us as we walked, and I didn't know what to make of it. I had fans when I sang in Nashville, but it had never felt like this. Even though I was singing, it'd felt empty because the people I was singing to were all strangers.

Tonight it had been with one of the men I loved while the other two listened, and that felt magical.

Simon and Zane stood, pulling us both into hugs and giving me a kiss, much to the amusement of the people around us. At least they weren't gaping at me. That had happened a few times at home.

"That was amazing, Lenn. You have got to do the competition in the next city."

"I don't know." I shrugged, even though inside, it didn't feel as scary as before. I guess having people who loved you and supported you made things feel less frightening.

When Slade grunted, I looked up and found his eyes searing into mine. He grabbed my chin, pulling me closer to him. "You deserve to be on stage, Peach. So, if I have to suffer through it to make you do it, then I will. It wasn't as bad having you singing to me."

"Yeah?" I asked, licking my lips. His possessiveness was sending a different vibe straight to my clit.

"Yeah." He smiled, leaning in to give me a kiss.

"Not bad, *hick*," a voice I was beginning to hate said, pulling me out of my loved-up bubble.

Slade growled, turning to face the guy that had dissed us the day before at the convention. "You following us, Lee?"

The man threw his head back, laughing as though

Slade had just told the funniest joke. If you knew Slade, that was funny within itself. The man did not joke. Lee fake wiped his eyes before settling on us again.

"You might do okay with this crowd, but you wouldn't stand a chance in the competition. Inkjection and Chopz have this thing in the bag. We've been teaming up for karaoke for the past two years, and no one has been able to take our crown. You might have won a few awards today, but in the end, it will be us standing on that podium."

It was then I realized he had backup this time, one of the snooty hairdressers and a scary girl who was cracking her knuckles as she looked us over. Slade was fuming next to me, and it would be any moment before he erupted, and we were kicked out of this nice place. I would even garner that Lee wanted that. I'd dealt with bullies my whole life, and the way to win was to not give in to their ploy. Acting unaffected, I rolled my eyes and picked up my drink, and slurped the rest of the fruity cocktail down.

"I don't know what is sadder. The only thing you have is winning this competition or your tattoo designs? Now, we're here enjoying an evening, which doesn't include you. Please see yourself out before I get on my new best friend here and alert them to rude guests."

I held up my phone, opening the app with the icon already pressed. Lee's face turned red, and I could tell he wanted to respond, so I began to count down.

"And five, four, three, two..."

His posse turned and stormed off before I got to one, and I sat the phone down as the guys sputtered, looking at me like I was some weird creature they'd never encountered before.

"What? I didn't lie. I wasn't going to throw down a challenge. I haven't heard them sing. I always hate that in movies when they get ahead of themselves. Plus, it's what they wanted. We don't need a competition to tell us we're better than them." I shrugged, picking up a fried mushroom and tossing it in my mouth.

"Does that thing let you pay your bill?" Slade asked, looking at my phone.

"Uh, yeah. Right here." I showed him the screen, and he took it from me, entering his card information quickly before pocketing my phone and standing. As soon as we were out of the bar, he picked me up, my legs going around his waist.

"Um, why are you carrying me?" I asked, not really hating the gesture. I was glad I'd opted to wear leggings today though, so my butt wasn't exposed.

"Because your legs are too short."

Simon snorted next to him, but shrugged. "He's not wrong, Lenn. And your whole speech back there has gotten us all ready to show you how amazing we think you are. Especially after you guys sang." He winked at me, licking his lips, and that was when I felt the hard length against my core.

"Oh!"

The guys chuckled and, in the next few seconds, we were back in the hotel and heading back to the room where Simon, Slade, and Zane showed me how much they loved me and my crazy mouth.

Chapter Fifteen

LENNOX

THE MORNING HAD BEEN SPENT packing and getting the details for the next convention. Simon offered to take care of it all when he and Zane decided to go for a walk. Zane had wanted to get some pictures of things when it wasn't as busy, and Simon had some shopping he wanted to do. It gave me time to call my parents and touch base with them.

"How are you doing, pumpkin?" my dad asked.

"Good. I'm experiencing so many new things. I never realized how much I was missing out on."

"I'm glad that you're getting out there. Your mom never wanted you to stay home the way you did."

"I know." I rubbed my forehead, knowing I'd taken on too much because of my mother's illness.

At the time, it had felt necessary. But now, even I

could admit it had become an unintentional crutch. Noah was a teenager, and Mom was doing so much better on her new medication. She was aware of her triggers, and we had enough support in place to help her.

I spent a few more minutes telling my dad about SIT, the places we'd seen so far, and the amazing food I'd gotten to try. I conveniently left out the person who'd stolen my wallet. No need to worry my dad.

"That's so good, pumpkin. I miss you and love you lots. Here's your brother. He wants to talk to you."

"Okay, Dad. Love you." I air-kissed the phone before he handed it over to my little brother. Noah's face came into view, and I instantly smiled bigger.

"Hey, Sis. Guess what?" He smiled at me, wiggling his eyebrows in excitement.

"What?" I made a funny face at him while I waited.

"I got first place at robotics camp."

"What? You did! That's awesome!"

Noah went on to tell me how he made his robot and the fight they had. When I got off the phone a while later, Slade stood against the wall, watching me.

"You miss them."

I nodded, wiping away a little tear. "I do, but not like I thought I would. I guess being in Nashville helped. I got used to not being there for every little thing. I still miss not knowing things the instant they happen, but it doesn't mean I'm not included or important. I'm getting to have my own experiences just as they are."

Slade walked over, scooping me into his arms and sitting back on the bed with me in his lap. I laid my head on his chest, finding my favorite spot. He kissed my hair, sighing contentedly as we sat there.

"I'm glad that you're here, Peach. It's also been good for me to remember how fun it can be to do things."

"I couldn't imagine doing any of them without y'all."

"You could, but I'm glad you aren't."

We sat for a few minutes before I broached the topic he'd been avoiding. "You nervous about seeing your dad… or meeting his girlfriend?" I asked, tilting my head slightly so I could see his face.

Slade blew out a breath, dropping his eyes to mine. "Am I that readable?"

The corner of my mouth lifted, and I shrugged a shoulder. "I just know you, remember, *Blaze*?"

His eyes heated, and he bent to kiss my nose. "Yeah, you do, and I love you for it." He took a deep breath before meeting my eyes again. "Things with my dad have never been easy. It's gotten better over the past years, and I'm just worried that meeting this woman will reverse it all. What if she's a bitch, and he takes her side?"

Turning so I was straddling his lap, I cupped his stubbled face between my hands. "Oh, Tatzilla. I don't know this woman, but I'll always be on your side no matter what. So will your brother and Simon. You're not alone anymore. I think the little boy who wants his dad to choose him is speaking there. You're scared, but you don't have to be. Trust your relationship."

His hands landed on my hips as he stared into my eyes, rolling the words I said around. "Okay." With that one word, I watched a weight lift off his shoulders, and he sealed his lips to mine in a bruising kiss. The door beeped a moment later, stopping us from taking it further.

"Hey, lovers," Simon purred. "Check out my goodies. Lenn, I got this for you."

I moved off Slade's lap as he groaned, and I couldn't help but notice the bulge. Smirking, I turned to Si and fawned over the items he'd gotten me. Slade cleared his throat, grabbing all of our attention.

"Do you guys care if we make a detour and stop by our dad's house?"

Smiling, I shook my head, looking at the other two. Zane had a smile, happy that Slade wasn't fighting it anymore. He turned to me, mouthing, "thank you." Once we had everything packed, we checked out of the hotel. Of course, Lee and his minions were in the lobby, but we skirted around them, pretending we didn't see them. We'd deal with them in the competition, but I wasn't going to risk anything else by starting a turf war. They weren't worth our adventure.

Once everything was packed, Zane climbed in the back with me as Slade took the wheel. For the first thirty minutes, Zane showed me some of the pictures he'd taken and what he would put on the new website and social media.

"Wow, these are great."

His face blushed a little at the praise. "Thanks. It's just something fun."

"I couldn't do that for fun."

"Yeah, well." He shrugged, pushing it off, but I could see how much he also liked it.

I dropped it, for now, snuggling under his arm. I glanced out the window as another city was left behind.

"Thanks, Babs," I whispered before I pulled out

my book, and I lost myself in a world of dragons for the next few hours.

WE PULLED up to a blue house a few hours later. It was pretty, with various flower beds in front and more in hanging pots. A porch swing with pillows set off to one side and an old rocking chair to the other. Slade turned off the van, and we all sat there, waiting. He looked at the house, and I wondered if he expected it to do something.

Zane glanced at me, giving me a nudge. Leaning forward, I placed my hand on Slade's forearm. He jumped a little at the contact like he'd been in a daze, unaware we were still in the vehicle.

"Hey, you ready?"

Slade peered down at me, then at Simon, reaching across to grab his hand. "Yeah." He swallowed, nodding to himself. "Yeah."

Zane was the first one to open the door, springing the rest of us into action. It was quiet as we made our way up to the front door, nothing but the sounds of the birds and insects to greet us. Slade stopped when we made it up the two stairs onto the porch, staring at the rocking chair. He gulped again and lifted his hand to ring the doorbell. Simon and I were on either side of him, with Zane on my other. We stood firm as our foursome group as we waited.

When the door opened, a little girl stared back at us. She had dark curls that were askew and big brown eyes that stared at us. I waved at her, and she smiled, still looking at us.

"Kara," a woman's voice yelled from inside before rounding a corner and finding the child at the door with it opened. "Honey, I told you not to open the door." The woman bent down to kiss the girl before glancing up at us, her hand on the girl. She was of average height with short brown hair and looked to be in her fifties.

"Apologies, we're watching my granddaughter, and she's a bit mischievous at the best of times. Please, come in. You must be Paul's sons. Your father is around back at the grill."

She opened the door, gesturing us in. No one said anything, so I introduced myself first. "Hello, I'm Lennox. Zane, or I mean Thane and Slade's girlfriend. Well, Simon's too." Half laughing, half coughing, I stopped, then tried again. "I'm Lennox."

The woman stood frozen for a few seconds at my comments, but then laughed, reaching out her hand. "It's lovely to meet you, Lennox. What a wonderful name. I'm Mia."

Shaking it, I gestured to the three guys. "Simon, Slade, and Thane, but I call him Zane after an unfortunate stalker situation last year where the guy pretended to be Thane, so, yeah."

I'd give it to Mia for her grace. She smiled, taking in what I'd blurted with no judgment. The guys behind me snorted, doing nothing to help me out.

"Well, I'm glad that's taken care of, and you're okay, dear. It's nice to finally meet you, both." She held out her hand to Zane first, who took it with ease.

"It's nice to meet you finally as well. Dad's talked about you so much, I feel like I already know you."

"Same." She smiled, dropping his hand to offer it to Slade. "Slade, I know things haven't been easy with you and your father, so I'm glad you were able to make time to visit. You'll find he's changed a lot in his old age."

"Humph," Slade grunted but shook her hand. "Thank you for inviting us for dinner." He lifted his eyebrow at me after dropping her hand, almost like he was reminding me he could have manners when he wanted to.

"And Simon. It's lovely to meet you as well." She peered at the four of us, smiling. "I'm not sure how your relationship works, but I want you to know that you're all welcome here. I'm so glad to have you and finally meet Paul's sons."

She smiled at them, and I could tell she loved the twin's father, making me happy that we'd taken the time to stop.

"And this is Kara?" I asked, dropping down to the little girl. She nodded, biting her lip as she watched me. "Well, Kara, I think we'll be best friends. Do you like to draw?"

She nodded enthusiastically, a smile lighting her face. Quicker than I could follow, she began to tell me all about her favorite crayons, dropping her grandmother's hand to tug on mine and led me to the table out back.

A man at the grill turned as we exited the house, and I could instantly see where Slade and Zane got their looks. The man might be in his mid-fifties, but he was very attractive. He was as tall as my boyfriends, with broad shoulders and muscular arms. His dark brown hair was peppered with just a little bit of gray, and he had a nice beard. He smiled when he saw me, placing the pair of tongs down on the side.

"You must be Lennox."

"My friend," Kara said, looking at me. Paul made his way over to us, a soft smile on his face for the little girl. I waved at him, smiling before laughing at Kara. I messed with her curls as she giggled.

"Of course, sweetie. Now, where are those crayons you were telling me about?"

She took me to the table just as the guys followed us out of the house. Zane went to his father, offering him a big hug with a few slaps on the back. I watched as they broke apart, and Paul turned to Slade. His smile never faded, and I hoped that Slade noticed it too. His dad loved him as much as he did Thane, no matter how it might have seemed when they were younger.

Simon stood next to Slade, and when he didn't move forward, Simon did, introducing himself. "Hello, sir. I'm Simon."

"It's nice to meet you, Simon." Paul shook his hand before looking at his son.

"Slade, I'm so glad you could make it. It means a lot to me." I couldn't be sure, but his dad's eyes looked a bit misty as he spoke.

Slade's face finally softened, and he stepped forward, wrapping his tattooed arms around him. They stood that way for a while, and I tried not to watch, but I couldn't help it, wiping a tear as I did. Mia patted my arm as she sat a few glasses of lemonade on the table. I'd been so preoccupied with the reunion I hadn't noticed her.

"Your hair is pretty," Kara said, looking up at me with big eyes.

"Thank you. Simon did it. He's great at doing hair stuff. I bet if you asked him, he'd do something cool with yours."

The little girl looked over at Simon, who smiled softly at her. He pretended to think about it. "Hmm, you know what, I could put a pink streak in it? Would that be okay?" he asked Mia, who sat down. "It's washable," he whispered when she looked between him and Kara.

"Please, grammy," Kara began to beg.

"Hmm, pink hair means you eat all your vegetables. You able to do that?"

"Savage," I whispered, chuckling.

Kara nodded, jumping up and down. "Yes. I promise."

"I guess I'll be right back," Simon said, winking. He walked around to the front of the house with Kara following him, and I glanced around, finding Slade at the grill with his dad, talking. Zane sat down in Kara's vacated seat, wrapping an arm around me.

"Have I told you how amazing you are?" he asked, kissing my neck.

"Hmm, I'm sure I'm due for another." Smiling, I looked up at him before going back to the crayons. Zane talked with Mia about her job while I colored the picture I'd started, humming along to the song in my head. As I tapped my foot, the feeling from last night of being on stage with Slade emerged, and I knew I wanted to do it again. I'd never felt that before. I'd always been more scared of messing up to focus on how alive it made me feel.

"You sing, Lennox?" Mia asked, startling me.

"Just for fun," I said, so used to replying that way, but it no longer felt right.

"We're trying to talk her and Slade into doing a singing competition. It's part of SIT that we're traveling around with through LiveIt."

"Oh, that sounds fun. You should do it while you're still young. Life has a way of speeding by."

I didn't know if she was speaking from experience, but I couldn't deny it was sound advice. A few minutes later, Kara and Simon came out the backdoor, her curls subdued and a bright pink streak in the front of her hair.

"Oh, I love it!" I exclaimed, getting up to preen over her. She smiled, lifting her head high as we all admired it.

"Dinner's about ready," Paul yelled, turning from the grill and spurring us into motion. I walked inside with Mia, Zane, and Simon following. She smiled, handing us plates, sides, and utensils. We carried it all out in one go, setting it on the table just as the burgers, ribs, and chicken were placed.

"I didn't know what you liked, so I made a bit of everything," Paul said, and if I wasn't mistaken, with a slight red tint to his cheeks.

"It looks amazing, Dad," Zane said.

"Yeah, I don't know what to take," I said, filling my plate with everything. Everyone began to eat, the table quiet as we munched on the delicious food.

"So, Lennox, I hear you're a tattoo artist like Slade?"

"Oh, yes, sir. Though, it took him forever to give me a chance," I teased.

"And Simon, you're a barber?"

"Technically, I'm unemployed at the moment. But yes, I work with hair. Do you need a trim?"

His dad laughed, shaking his head. "No, but thanks for the offer."

"How are the shops going?" his dad asked, directing the question to Slade this time.

"I've reopened the Kentucky store. It's having a soft opening while we're away, and we'll do a full opening once we're back. It's doing well, though. I'm looking for another location while we're out here."

"Oh, any prospects?"

"We've been to St. Louis and Branson, both lovely,

but they didn't have that spark I was looking for. We have a few more cities to go to."

"Memphis isn't far from here," Mia piped up, a hopeful look on her face.

"Yeah, that's our next stop," Zane said. "You guys should come by the convention if you have time. See them all in action."

"Oh? Is that tomorrow?"

"Yeah. But you don't have to. I know how important your job is," Slade answered quickly.

"I think I could take the day off."

Mia smiled at Paul, patting his hand. "Yeah, I think that would be nice."

"If you're serious, I can see about getting you tickets. I'll have them hold them at the booth."

Paul looked at Slade, who'd suddenly focused on his burger, finding it fascinating, and I realized how much of that little boy who was scared of being rejected by his father was still present. I squeezed his hand, giving him my strength.

"Yeah, we'll be there," Paul said, making me like him just a little bit more. Though, if he failed to show up tomorrow, he'd be on my list, and my daddy had taught me how to shoot a gun and dispose of a body.

"What about bodies?" Simon whispered, leaning over.

My face flushed when I realized I'd been saying it aloud.

The rest of the meal was pleasant, and I could see some cracks in Slade's armor repairing right before my eyes. After we cleaned up, we left with hugs and a few pictures that Kara had drawn us. And I prayed that nothing would keep Paul from attending tomorrow. Slade's heart depended on it.

Chapter Sixteen

SIMON

WHEN I HEARD the door open and close early in the morning, I wasn't surprised to find the spot next to me empty. Slade was chasing some demons, and when his mind was this full, he struggled to sleep. With the convention later today and his father's impending attendance weighing on him, I had an idea where he was. Only a few things made his thoughts clear, and at this hour, that meant one thing —the gym.

But I had a feeling it wouldn't be enough. Not this time. Crawling out of bed, I silently dressed, grabbing a few things as I made my way to the door.

"Si?" Lennox whispered, her voice soft with sleep.

"Hey baby, I'm right here." I leaned down on the bed, kissing her forehead.

"Slade?" she asked, blinking her eyes, trying to open them.

"I'm going to take care of him."

"Okay. He needs you," she mumbled, patting my hand before giving up the fight with her eyes and leaving them closed. Smiling, I kissed her lips and headed toward the door.

Some days, I still didn't quite believe this was my life. That I got to have both of the people I loved in it. Thane being added had given me a brother, and I loved our dynamic altogether. We were a family, and it was more than I ever imagined.

Stepping out into the hallway, I quietly shut the door behind me, hoping they could get some more sleep. I was jazzed up as it was, hoping today would be a turning point for me. Memphis' competition was a little different with categories you could compete in, and there was one for stage makeup that I was excited about. I wanted to branch out and do more with my skills, and this was the perfect place to do it.

The thrill of creating something zipped through me as I jogged down the stairs, humming a song under my breath as I descended the floors. When I got to the bottom marked with the fitness room, I pulled out my card and swiped it, heading in the direction the sign pointed. There weren't any other people up yet since it was around four in the morning. Most people were still snuggled in their beds at this hour, which helped with my plan.

The fitness room loomed ahead, and as I hoped, there was one lone tattooed figure inside. Swiping my card again, I slid into the room, leaning against the door for a moment while I watched the muscles flex in his back. He was staring off into the distance as he lifted weights, his earbuds in, and hadn't noticed my arrival yet.

Ninety percent of the time, with Slade and me, he was the more dominant one. But every now and then, he needed me to dominate him and force him out of his own head. And I believed this was one of those occasions.

Stalking forward, I hit the lights, casting the room into darkness. He tensed, but before he could turn around, I grabbed his earbud out and leaned close to him. His tattoos already shone with sweat, his chest heaving as he tried to catch his breath. At my touch, he stilled, relaxing.

"Did you think you could sneak out of bed, and I wouldn't notice?" I whispered, grabbing his hips and pulling him to me. I licked his neck, tasting the salt on his skin. I growled when he didn't answer, nicking my teeth against his flesh. "Answer."

"Yes," he said, gulping. Slade's body began to

vibrate, proving even more that he needed me to take control and get him out of his head.

"Good thing I find your stubbornness hot, babe. But you need to stop fighting your battles alone." My hands snaked around, trailing over the band of his shorts. His happy trail teased me, and I flattened my hand onto his abs, enjoying how they felt beneath my fingers. I rocked my hips into him, my own arousal evident as it found the space between his ass cheeks. A whimper left him at the motion, inching my own lust higher.

Giving into what he needed, I slipped my hand below his shorts, finding his cock waiting for me. Slade's head fell back onto my shoulder as I stroked him, squeezing him tight. As I rubbed my thumb over the slit, the tip was already leaking.

"More," he wheezed, panting into my neck, his eyes meeting mine. They were blown, and I could see the relief in them that I'd come to him.

"Did you forget how this works? You do as I say. And I'm not done playing yet."

He nodded, biting his lip to moan as I tugged his cock harder, slowly drawing my hand down his length. His eyes rolled back, and he squeezed them shut.

"You have two choices," I said, pulling back. I'd decided my plan when I saw how desperate he was for me. I was all for living on the edge and grabbing a handful of his junk in this public space, but I didn't fancy being caught balls deep in him and chance getting kicked out of the hotel before the convention even started. "I can jerk you off here, and then we can go back to the room with breakfast…"

"Or?" he asked, his eyes opening to look at me when I didn't finish. Smirking, I rolled my thumb over his dripping slit again.

"Or, we can move this to the room, and I can own your ass while Lennox sucks you off."

Slade whimpered, his cock jumping in my hand at the thought, but I needed him to say it. Not once since we'd been together as a group had he let me take him with an audience. For some reason, it was too vulnerable for him. I didn't know if it was because of his brother or Lennox, but something always stopped him from crossing that line when it was all of us.

"Ro-om," he panted, opening his eyes. Smiling at his bravery, I kissed him, pulling my hand out of his shorts.

"Good choice," I said, praising him for being brave.

He quickly fixed his shorts and grabbed his shirt off the bench he'd placed it on. We both exited the room in a flash, and I could tell he was close to bursting; the complete submission was a high for him, and he was chasing it. Thankfully, the elevator arrived quickly, and I hit the button for our floor. I stood far away from him, too worried we wouldn't make it to the room if our skin touched at all. We were live wires, waiting to explode on contact.

An eternity later, the door opened, and we bolted out, racing to our room. Laughing, I pulled out my key card, swiping it in the door. We tumbled in, and I regained control, pressing him against the wall. Slade went willingly, his hips rocking forward to meet mine. Taking his mouth, I delivered an aggressive kiss, our tongues waging a battle. Nipping his lip, I drew back, staring him in the eyes.

"Hands and knees on the bed. Go see if you can stir our other lover."

Slade swallowed, and I grabbed him outside his shorts, squeezing. He groaned, his body trembling with need, and he nodded.

"Yes," he rasped, licking his lips.

Slade kicked off his shoes and toed off his socks as he went, dropping his shirt and shorts before he turned the corner. His tattooed backside beckoned me, and I groaned, rubbing a hand down my face. Pulling my clothes off, I grabbed the bottle of lube and a plug from my suitcase.

When I made it to the bed, I found Slade's beautiful ass perched high in the air as he kneeled on the bed. His hands roamed Lennox as he stirred her, and they began to kiss, lost in the moment. Rubbing my hands over his backside, I drizzled some lube on his hole, loving how it puckered at the sensation. Coating the plug in it, I slowly began to prep Slade.

Since I didn't top him very often, I had to prepare him more, and I found the plug worked better to get him there. I was half tempted to make him wear it all day, but since we had things to do, I wouldn't. But the thought crossed my mind, bringing a smirk to my face.

Focusing back on the job at hand, I squeezed some on my own cock, groaning at the contact. Leaning forward, my front met his back as I reached down and squeezed him. He moaned into his kiss, his hands working in Lennox's pussy as she writhed on the bed. Thane had woken as well, his hand covering her breasts as he kissed and nipped at her neck.

Pulling back, I began to fuck Slade with the plug, his legs trembling from the sensation. When he felt ready, I pulled it out, watching as his hole stretched and quivered for me.

"Lennox, hands, and knees. Suck Slade while Thane fucks you from behind," I ordered. The other two stopped what they were doing, eagerly obeying what I said, and got into position. Slade moaned when her lips wrapped around his cock, and I grabbed his neck, pulling his head to me.

"How does it feel to surrender, babe?" I whispered, edging my cock into him.

"So good," he wheezed as I let go, spreading his cheeks so I could push the rest of the way in. Once I was fully seated, I gripped his hips, holding him. His body was trembling again, and I moved one of my hands back to his throat, taking control.

"You ready?" I asked, and he nodded, the only movement he could manage as I began to pull out and slam back into him. I watched his tattoos move, trying not to focus on how tight his backside was. When I felt him begin to tense up, I knew he was close to erupting. Letting go of his throat, I smoothed a hand down his spine before gripping his hip tight, hoping to leave little fingerprints to remind him he'd been owned by me.

With a breath, I slid in and out, grunting each time I bottomed out in him. When I hit his p-spot just right, he came with a roar, and I watched as Lennox swallowed him down. She licked her lips, letting him fall out once she had her fill, and Thane pulled her back, moving in and out of her quicker.

Pushing Slade down to the bed, I focused on my release, feeling it close. Throwing my head back, I thrust into Slade one more time, unable to hold it back. My balls drew up, and I shouted as I released everything into him.

"Shit," he cursed, his legs quivering from the force. Once I was done, I slowly pulled out, walking to the bathroom to clean the plug and grab something for him. He lay panting on the bed, watching Lennox as she came apart around his twin.

Carefully, I wiped him down, giving him the care he always did for us. When I crawled back into bed a few minutes later, I pulled him into my arms, kissing his shoulder. He didn't fight me being the bigger spoon, letting me stay top for a bit longer.

As Lennox and Thane settled down, he tilted his head back, looking me in the eyes. They were clearer now; his demons successfully chased for the moment. He kissed my lips softly.

"Thank you, Fish."

I smoothed my hand over his cheek, kissing him back. "Always, babe."

Glancing at the time, I saw we still had a few hours before we needed to be up, so I closed my eyes, snuggling back into bed, knowing there was nowhere else I ever wanted to be if these three people weren't there.

Chapter Seventeen

LENNOX

WE'D ALREADY BEEN GREETING and mingling with people for an hour, and we still had an hour to go before we selected our contestant. The Memphis crowd was a lot different than Branson. For one thing, the venue was bigger, meaning there was a larger crowd. There were more booths, too, meaning more competitors. I recognized some of the studios from the last one, but there were a lot of new ones making me a little uneasy.

"You'll be fine," Slade said, pulling me to sit on his lap. I went willingly, finding comfort in his arms.

"It's just a lot more people." I shrugged, watching onlookers walk by. Our tables hadn't had as big of a crowd today, and I wondered if Inkjection had anything to do with it. They were two booths ahead of us and were standing out, catching people as they walked by, giving them temporary tattoos.

"I don't like that guy," I said, narrowing my eyes at the back of Lee.

"He's a douche. Just ignore him," Slade said, brushing my hair off my shoulder. "I think I should change your name to watermelon for the summer, Peach."

Giggling, I looked back at him, finding him focused on me. "You like this hair color?"

He nodded, kissing the nape of my neck. This morning felt like days ago. I'd been surprised to see Simon in charge, but I knew that Slade had needed someone to take his mind off things. He'd been less grouchy as well since and more of the teddy bear I knew him to be. Well, when he wanted.

"It suits you," he said. He dropped his head on my shoulder, and I turned back to the crowd. I knew if I didn't stop, I'd lose myself in his eyes and forget everyone else. It wasn't a bad thing, but I wanted to rein in my lust since we were in public.

"No thanks, my son is the best tattoo artist I know," a familiar voice said at Inkjection's booth seconds before Paul appeared.

"Dad," Slade said, standing, almost forgetting I was sitting in his lap, catching me at the last second.

"You came." His voice hitched a little, and I could feel the relief in his body.

His dad smiled, nodding with pride as he took in our booth. "Hey Lennox, it's good to see you again." I moved out from behind the table, giving him a hug. Mia was with him, so I hugged her, glad they'd shown up.

"This is amazing," Mia said, looking around at everything. "When does the competition portion start?" she asked.

"In a few hours. The meet and greet part finishes in about thirty minutes, and then we pick our clients and work on the design. The hair competition takes place during that time, and then ours. There's more overlap here since the style section is larger."

"Wow, I never knew something like this existed. It's incredible." Mia smiled kindly, genuine awe in her voice, making me like her even more. Even if we didn't win or find some great treasure, this road trip would be a success alone from Slade mending this relationship.

"Do you have a lot of people to choose from?" Paul asked, looking thoughtful.

"Not as many as last time. We've been tattoo-blocked by another studio," Slade said, shooting his eyes to Lee, who'd been watching us.

"Ah, I see. I guess rivalry is everywhere. Where

does one sign up?" his dad asked, and I think Slade about had a stroke from it. He stared at him like he wasn't sure he was hearing his dad correctly.

Picking up the clipboard, I handed it to his dad, showing him where to sign his name. He gave it back to Slade, who blinked down at it. He gulped, nodding as he held it to his chest.

"Well, we're going to look around a few other places. We'll stop by later. Can we bring you some food?" Mia asked.

"That would be great. Thank you." I hugged her again, and she squeezed my hand before they walked off, Slade still standing silently.

"You ok, Tatzilla?" I asked, taking his hand. He peered down at me, his eyes a little misty.

"My dad wants me to give him a tattoo."

"You sure it wasn't me he requested?" I teased, causing him to break out of his stance as he smiled at me.

"Oh, you think you're funny, huh?" Slade bent down, kissing me, his shock wearing off. He pulled the clipboard back, and I laughed, knowing he was double-checking it was his name.

"What does he want?" I asked, trying to peer at the sheet.

"He put artist choice." He looked at me, swallowing. "Well, I guess I know who I'm tattooing. Do you have any contenders?"

"There were two I was considering." I grabbed the list, and we walked around to the chairs. I placed it out in front of me, scanning it. When I saw the two, I pointed, watching as he considered them. One was a constellation down a spine, and the other was a dream catcher on a thigh. Slade tapped the pen against the table, his tell that he was designing something in his head.

I was about to place a pad under his pen so he could sketch out what he envisioned when he pointed to the dream catcher. "It's more intricate and will show your skill more."

Smiling, I kissed his cheek, pulling out my phone to send them a message. When I glanced back, he had his notebook, already sketching an outline for his dad. I knew he didn't care about the competition with this one and would make it meaningful.

Since he was preoccupied, I also began to work on my own. We were both lost in our sketches when someone approached. I was in the zone and figured they were just looking at our portfolio, so I didn't stop what I was doing.

"You have skill. You should leave this mediocre studio and join mine. It's far superior."

The voice shocked me, so I glanced up, finding

Lee staring down at me, a mean-looking girl with him, and I felt Slade tense next to me.

"I'm good, thanks." I dropped my eyes, hoping they'd leave now that I'd said something, but he continued to stare.

"Seriously." He leaned down, getting into my space.

Sighing, I placed my stuff down, feeling Slade vibrating next to me. He was two seconds away from punching this man and ruining his opportunity with his dad. Stepping in front of him, he pulled me into his body, holding me to his chest. It didn't matter, though. It worked to keep him from lashing out at the stupid jerk in front of me.

"Sweetie, I've tried to be nice. But maybe I need to spell this out for you clearer. This isn't the school playground where you can insult me and make me want to work for you. I'm not a toy for you to win away from Slade. Tattooed Hearts is more than just a parlor to me. It's *my* heart. Slade and I have a bond that transcends anything else. Nothing you offer me will ever measure up to the love, belonging, and pride I have every day when I work with the man I love. Now, please, vacate our area and stick to your own."

His eyes heated with embarrassment, and I realized we'd drawn a crowd, but I didn't care. I was tired of him trying to bait us. "Bye, now." I waved him off, sitting back into Slade's lap, his arms circling me more. I felt him chuckling into my back as he hid his face.

Lee's face was bright red, but he pulled away, stalking off, knocking a few things down as he did. The girl sneered at me before following. I waved at them, not caring, just hoping they'd stay gone this time.

"Peach, have I told you how much I love your sass?"

"Hmm?" I tapped my mouth, pretending to think about it. "I think you told me you hated it, actually."

"Never," he growled, his fingers tightening, sending shivers down me. "It's one of my favorite things. Especially when you use that mouth to suck me off," he whispered, making my breath catch. Rubbing my legs together, I slapped his arm, knowing he was trying to distract himself, but I wasn't really one to be horny around a crowd of people right before I had to take a tattoo gun to someone.

Standing, I narrowed my eyes at him as I moved back to my seat. "If you want to ever experience it again, then I'd keep it controlled, *sir*."

His eyes heated, and I realized I'd just poked him even more. Turning, my cheeks reddened as I tried to focus back on the drawing on my page. I had a dream catcher sketched in no time, and I was tweaking it when Mia and Paul returned with food.

"We got a little bit of everything," Mia said, setting down some plates. Simon and Zane were behind them, grinning as they caught my attention.

Slade stayed in his own bubble, drawing something I couldn't see. He'd covered his arm over it, leaning so no one could catch a glimpse of the page. While he worked, I chatted with his dad and Mia, Simon telling us what he would do for the makeup portion of the competition this time.

"It was amazing, Lenn. Everyone kept asking me about your hair, saying how much they loved it," he gushed.

I swished it back and forth, loving how it felt. "Well, it is fantastic." I blew him a kiss, loving that he was getting recognized. Before I knew it, it was time for his competition, and he gave me a kiss for luck as he strolled away. Mia decided to go with him, wanting to watch him work.

"You ready, Noxy girl?" Zane asked me.

"Yeah, I am." He nodded toward his brother, a question in his eyes. I shifted my eyes to his dad, and he understood.

Slade suddenly stood, walked over to his chair, and began to prep. I'd only seen him this singularly focused once before, and that was when he tattooed me. When he had everything ready, he looked up, realizing we'd all been watching.

"Dad, you ready?"

"Oh, is it time?" he asked, walking over.

"Yes, for you, it is." He didn't say anything else, but I could see all of his hopes and fears as he waited for his dad to take a seat.

"Do I get to see it?" his dad asked.

"I'd rather you waited until the end."

His dad assessed him, considering something before he nodded. Settling back as he rolled up his shirt sleeve. Slade immediately fell into his professional role, transferring the design to his skin. He looked at it, smiling, before pulling out his gun and beginning. He watched his dad as he made contact, relaxing when he didn't jump up off the table. Zane moved over and started to talk to his dad, distracting him.

Slade didn't even seem to hear when the announcer came on, stating that our competition would be starting. Carol arrived, and I showed her the design. Together we made a few tweaks before I printed it off. Once I had her in the chair, I zoned out, losing myself in the process.

When the time ended a few hours later, my body was tight from being in one position for so long. I sat back, stretching my fingers as I looked at the tattoo. We'd weaved bits of color and shadowing into it, and I loved how it had turned out.

"I love it," she gushed, pulling me into a hug. Patting her arm, I looked around, seeing we'd drawn a crowd.

That was when I realized it was for Slade's tattoo. I wanted to gasp at its beauty, but I didn't want to disturb him as he finished. It was one of the most intricate designs I'd ever seen him do. It was a story about him, his dad, his mom, and his brother. There were things to represent them all: a baseball, daisies, airplanes, and roads that ran down the middle with some state signs of where they'd lived. There were even the stars and letters we'd written. It was beautiful, and I hoped his dad would appreciate it. It covered his entire bicep. How he'd completed it in four hours was a testament to his commitment.

He stood back, handing his dad a mirror. He looked at it, his eyes shiny with tears as he took in the details. When he'd taken in all angles of it, catching all the small details, he looked at Slade, and I wondered if he was seeing him for the first time.

"It's magnificent, Son." Paul pulled Slade into his arms, holding him tight.

Zane placed his arm around me, pulling me into his embrace, and I knew he was also feeling emotional. For so long, he'd been the bridge between the two, stuck in the middle of his family.

When they pulled apart, the crowd clapped at his design as Paul showed it off to the onlookers. When I spotted Lee in the crowd, his gaze narrowed, and I knew he was up to something. So, it was no surprise when the LiveIt official came around and stated that since Slade had started early, he was disqualified from the overall scoring for this competition but could still win one of the local categories that were voted on by the crowd. Slade didn't even care, shrugging his shoulder. He'd done it for his dad, not the competition.

"Lee said something," I grumbled to Zane, looking up at him as Mia and Simon returned full of smiles. "He's going to be a problem. We need to do something."

Zane nodded before we hugged Simon and Mia. As a group, we walked over to the stage area as they began to announce the awards. It took them a while to get through the hair and makeup, and I was starting to lose hope when Simon hadn't been announced yet. He shuffled his feet as well, trying to hide his disappointment.

"For overall makeup and hair, the award goes to Simon Fisher."

Jumping up and down, I grabbed his hands as he

stood speechless. "Go, Simon!" Pushing him toward the stage, he stumbled up there as his volunteer modeled her hair and makeup. I realized she looked like a mermaid, and I loved the look.

He came back with a broad smile, and I saw how people started looking at him differently. Holding his hand, I was ready to go when they started announcing the tattoo awards.

"We don't have to stay. We can find out later," I said after half had been called.

"No, we're staying," Slade said, giving me a look.

"In first place, we have Lennox from Tattooed Hearts."

I stared, confident I'd dreamed them saying my name. This time it was Simon who nudged me, smiling as I stumbled my way up to the podium. The picture of my dream catcher was on the screen. Taking the paper, I waved as I returned, my cheeks heating at the attention.

"Next, we have an honorable mention due to some time limits being out of the norm, but a crowd favorite," the announcer said, casting their eyes. "Otherwise, this tattoo would've won overall." They cleared their throat before announcing Slade's name.

He rolled his eyes but walked up there, taking the award from them. I watched Lee the whole time, happy when he seemed mad that Slade had still won something.

It was no surprise when Inkjection was then awarded overall. No one applauded for them, though, and I wondered if everyone had heard what he'd done. It gave me some satisfaction if they did.

"Do you have to leave?" Slade asked his dad and Mia.

Mia looked at Paul, then back at the group. "I don't know about you guys, but I'm famished. What if we grabbed something to eat? I know a place."

With a round of nods, we followed them out, and we had another family dinner. But this one was filled with laughs, and I knew that Slade's relationship with his father had mended through the power of a tattoo.

Chapter Eighteen

LENNOX

"PLEASE FILL in all the space up to the rope," the woman leading the tour said, directing people. I stopped, staring at the room we were currently viewing at Graceland, the home of Elvis Presley. It had been a unanimous vote to visit.

"This room was the sitting room where Elvis would greet a lot of his guests."

It was decked out in mostly white with blue accents, the blue velvet curtains being a huge eye-catcher. It had white carpet and a massive white couch that apparently sat fifteen people. But what stood out to me were the stained glass windows that adorned a door. A brilliant peacock design was displayed, creating a kaleidoscope of color across the room. Just beyond the windows sat a piano, and I could imagine Elvis sitting there, playing.

"Wow," Zane breathed as we both looked around. We kept walking, entering the dining room next.

"Interesting fact," the lady said, "Elvis owned fourteen TVs, which for the '50s was very extravagant." She pointed to the old tube TVs I'd seen in my grandparents' house on display. It sat in the corner near the table where the family could watch while they ate.

"Fourteen TVs is still extravagant," Slade whispered, causing me to laugh. We kept walking, taking in everything as we followed the crowd.

"This is the Jungle Room which is unique in that it has carpet on the ceiling and floor, providing excellent acoustics. Elvis recorded parts of two albums here, making it historical as well."

"Jungle is definitely a good word for this room," Simon said, taking in the green carpet, wood-paneled walls, and plant decor.

The tour guide smiled, continuing her speech. "It was designed with a Polynesian feel to remind Elvis of Hawaii, a place he loved."

Simon's face reddened, and he ducked his head as we continued. Slade nudged him, giving him a look, and I had to contain a giggle that wanted to slip through. As the tour guide walked us through Elvis' final day, we made it through the house and moved on to some of the outer buildings. It was sad to think of such a legend dying the way he did.

"This room holds all of the awards and gold records he's received since his death…"

"Whoa," I said, turning in a circle as I looked at the covered walls. There were even a few of the jumpsuits he wore on display. Simon shut my jaw as I stared at it all, making me laugh.

We finished the tour with his collection of cars, including the pink Cadillac and his personal airplane that we learned had velvet seats, gold seatbelts, and phones that could call anywhere in the world.

"Elvis was badass," Slade admitted as we finished the tour.

Smiling, I grabbed his hand, leaning into him as we walked. I wouldn't say that Slade had become an entirely different person overnight. He was still his grumpy, alpha-hole self, but there was a lightness to his eyes, and his smile was easier to spread.

"What's next?" Zane asked, looking back at us. We had the whole day to sightsee before leaving in the morning to travel to our next stop.

"The Sun Studio," I said, smiling. I was the most excited about this, and I wasn't entirely sure why, but something about it called to me.

"Sweet, let's hit up the gift shop and head there."

After buying too much stuff, we loaded up in the

van and headed toward the studio. It was quiet as we drove, all of us in our own thoughts, but it felt nice like we were all comfortable enough to think without feeling awkward in the silence.

Parking next to the building, I held my breath as I stared at Sun Studio. I didn't know why, but something about it felt magical. So many artists had gotten their start right here. It felt momentous.

Walking up, I almost fell over as I tried to take in the colossal guitar on the sign. It was the biggest guitar I'd ever seen. Slade took my hand, pulling me through the doors, or I might have stayed frozen outside of it, looking at all the photographs of the stars who'd recorded here.

The tour guide started to share how the studio started, but all I could hear was the whooshing in my ears as I looked around at the history of singers from Johnny Cash to U2. When the tour ended, I couldn't remember much of what was said, but a feeling had settled in me, one I was too afraid to admit out loud.

The guys looked at me, nervous at my silence, but I smiled, trying to distract them from asking me about it. "So, where to now? Maybe some food?"

The guys nodded, looking at one another, but let me get away with not talking for the moment. We spent the rest of the day touring the Crystal Shine

Grotto and the Blues Hall of Fame. By the time we got back to the hotel, I was tired and ready for a rest.

"I was thinking," Simon said as we entered the hotel room. "What if we nap and then go to the karaoke night?"

"You want to do that? I thought we'd decided not to engage with Lee?"

"We don't have to fight them to enjoy ourselves, and if you don't want to do the competition part, we could always just go to a bar and sing for fun. I saw your face today, Lenn. I know you're itching to sing something."

I chewed it over, thinking about what he was saying. The thought of facing off with Lee and his minions didn't sit well with me, but singing at a random place felt more my speed.

"Okay, a random place could be fun."

Simon rushed forward, grabbing me around the waist as he scooped me up and deposited me on the bed, tickling me. Eventually, we settled down, the anxious energy I'd been feeling fell away, and I was able to sleep, a smile on my face at what the night would hold.

SIMON HAD DECIDED he wanted to do my makeup for me, so I was now decked out with my watermelon hair and matching makeup. I didn't have a dress to match me, but the robin's-egg blue one went well with the whole ensemble. Stepping out into the room, Slade and Zane stopped their conversation to take me in. A loud whistle rang out as I turned, feeling like a beauty queen under their gazes.

"You look beautiful, Peach," Slade said, stepping toward me. He stopped before getting to me, taking in every detail head to toe. "Amazing work, Si." He lifted his eyes to the man behind me, a wicked smirk on his lips. "I'll have fun undressing her later."

"Hey now, brother. Sharing is caring."

Snorting, I grabbed my purse and headed toward the door, the giddiness of the evening taking over. "Come on, let's go sing. We can leave the sleeping arrangements for later."

The three of them followed me out, and we took off toward all the lights. Our hotel was close to a lot of entertainment, making it easy to find somewhere to go. Earlier I'd looked up a few I wanted to stop in at, so when the sign for Last Note Lounge came into view, I nearly skipped toward it.

"I've never seen you so eager to sing," Slade said, grabbing my hand.

"I know. There's just something about Memphis.

It's the birthplace of so many amazing stories, and maybe I thought it could be part of ours."

"Our story doesn't need any Memphis magic, Peach. It has you."

A blush began to cover me from head to toe as we stepped into the bar, the music greeting us before we even made it through the door. Already, I could feel it zipping through me, making me come alive.

Immediately, I dashed toward the stage where a man stood. He glanced up, eyeing my hair and makeup, and he didn't seem as impressed as my boyfriends had. "Yes?"

"I want to sing," I said, smiling wide as I practically bounced on my toes.

He let out a loud bellow, slapping his leg. I frowned, not understanding. "Oh, you're serious? Listen, doll, no one sings around here unless they've auditioned. Those are once a week, and the line is long to get through. Come back on Tuesday if you're serious, and we'll see if you can hack it." He eyed me up and down one more time, clearly not thinking I had what it took.

Feeling slightly dejected, I turned, almost running into Slade, who I hadn't realized was behind me. "Sorry, um, they're full," I mumbled, taking his hand to drag him away. He planted his feet, though, not moving. I looked up at his face, finding he was glaring at the man who'd laughed. He had on his classic alpha-hole face that made most men cry or crap their pants.

I felt embarrassed enough that I didn't want to get into it with this guy. I should've known there were auditions. I had to go through that in Nashville. Gripping his hand, I squeezed it, hoping he'd look down at me.

"Please, Tatzilla, let's just go somewhere else."

His jaw ticked, but he nodded, searing the guy behind me with one more look before he let me pull him away. Simon also had a scowl on his face, looking like he might charge the guy. Shaking my head, I pleaded to Zane to help me drag them without causing a scene. Nodding, he took his brother as I pushed Simon, tugging on his hand.

When we got outside, I tried to smile, bringing back some of the happiness I'd felt earlier. "There are a few other places we can try," I said, but I wasn't feeling hopeful. I was sure they were like this place—auditions required.

The guys grumbled but followed, our foursome quiet as we walked down the strip. The line to the second place was out the door, making me skip it altogether. Not feeling lucky, we ducked into the third place, and I had the guys sit at a table as I went to find whoever I needed to be rejected by.

A woman stood by a door to the back area, so I headed to her, ready to be told no. She smiled warmly at me, giving me a little hope.

"What can I do for you, darlin'?" she asked.

"I know this is a long shot, but do you have any openings to sing?"

She looked me over, but it felt different from the first guy. She wasn't finding me lacking but taking me in, curious. "Typically, no, but I had someone call out tonight. If you can go on in twenty, the spot is yours. I have a feeling about you."

I stood there, staring, feeling like she was pulling my leg. "Seriously?" I squeaked, my face finally catching on as I smiled widely at her.

"Yup. You can head backstage now to warm up."

Nodding, I turned back to the table, giving them a thumbs up. Walking through the door, I felt like I'd come home. The green room was filled with colorful signs and pictures of the artists that had performed here. One girl was off in the corner, tuning her guitar, and I sat down, feeling out of place.

"First time?" she asked, glancing up.

"Here? Yeah. Is it that obvious?" I laughed, wiping my sweaty palms on my dress.

"You have that fresh face look about you still. I'm Matilda."

"Lennox." I waved, smiling at her.

"If you need to warm up your pipes, go ahead." She went back to her guitar, humming as she strummed it.

"Tilda," someone shouted, and she stood, giving me a salute as she headed toward the stage. Once she was clear of the door, the guy turned to me. "I need your name and song," he said, looking up from his clipboard as he waited for my answer.

"Oh, um," I hesitated, debating if I wanted to use the last stage name or my real one. LJ Star didn't feel like me anymore. "Lennox James and I'll be singing, 'Change my Everything' by Shadows of Mayhem."

He scribbled it down before he nodded and walked out the door. Muted sounds from outside traveled through the walls, but for the most part, it was quiet, so I ran through some scales, warming up my voice.

When he came back a few minutes later, I was ready. Matilda smiled at me, patting my arm as she walked offstage and headed toward the bar. I stepped out under the lights, that sense of rightness returning. This was it.

The music started, and I opened my mouth, losing myself to the song.

Chapter Nineteen

THANE

THE MOMENT LENNOX stepped out onto the stage, it felt like everyone stopped and waited for her to shine. Or perhaps, it just seemed that way because it was how my heart operated, not really beating until she was there. She smiled at the crowd, waving as she approached the microphone.

The music began, and I watched as she took a deep breath, letting it flow through her whole body as she began to move. When the first word passed her lips, I was transfixed like I always was when she sang. Smiling at her song choice, I hummed along to the Shadows of Mayhem tune we'd been listening to all week while driving.

I didn't want to say it was our song, but it felt like it was.

"Yes," Simon cheered when the lights began to

dance across her makeup, and I realized he'd done it in a way for her to sparkle more under them.

"Wow, that's cool. I thought she looked gorgeous, but seeing her like that, it's like she's a magical creature or something."

My twin grunted next to me, but he didn't deny it. I peeked at him out of the corner of my eye, finding him watching her with a smile on his face. I pulled out my phone to record her so I could upload it later. I hadn't thought I'd enjoy documenting the trip as much as I actually did.

When it was over, it felt like all the magic was sucked out of the room as she left the stage. I wasn't sure, but it seemed like everyone else deflated with her exit too.

"Any chance we can convince her to do the karaoke competition?" Simon asked.

"I don't know. She's adamant she doesn't want to get into it with Lee."

Before we could discuss it any further, Lennox returned out the door with a massive smile on her face. There was someone new singing now, but they didn't have her charisma, and people had gone back to talking at their tables.

We stood when she neared, each of us wanting to congratulate her on the performance. Of course, my impatient brother had to be first.

"Peach, that was magnificent."

He kissed her, only letting her go so Simon could hug and congratulate her. I picked her up when she got to me, wanting to feel her close.

"Noxy girl, you sang our song. I loved it."

Her cheeks reddened as she smiled. "It felt right." I kissed her quickly, not wanting to create a scene, and sat her back on her feet. Simon had gone to get some drinks, so when he returned, I was surprised it was with an older woman.

"Um, Lenn, this woman wanted to meet you."

"Lennox, is it?" she asked, smiling as she held her hand to shake. Our girl nodded, standing to shake it.

"Hi." She smiled, looking at Simon, unsure why she was greeting this woman.

"My name is Shannon Clark, and I'm a talent scout for Songbird Entertainment. Have you heard of it before?" she asked, gesturing for us to take our seats. She sat next to Lennox, taking Slade's seat, and I admired her when she didn't seem intimidated by my brother and his intense stare.

"No, I don't think I have. We're not from around here. Is it a local thing?"

Shannon smiled, shaking her head. "No, and that's not uncommon to not know the name of the company. Basically, we group several bands or artists for a tour that we think would do well together, and they travel together to music festivals across the states. Some of our groups already have record deals, so this gives them a cheaper option to tour since we foot the bill. Other artists are just starting out, and it helps get them noticed."

"Okay, that sounds pretty cool. Why are you telling me this, though?" Her face held a look of curiosity and apprehension, like she was too scared to hope.

Shannon smiled kindly. "Because I think you'd be great to add to one of our current lineups. They had a band drop out, so there's an opening."

Lennox's jaw dropped open as she looked around at the table. "Did you guys put her up to this?" she asked, searching our eyes for the answer.

I held my hands up, shaking my head no. Simon did something similar, but Slade narrowed his eyes at her like it was the dumbest question she'd ever asked.

"I promise I'm not a joke. I'm not even supposed to be working. I was here visiting a friend when you came on. I don't know if you could see it from up there on stage, but the entire room stopped what they were doing to listen."

"They did?" Lennox asked, looking around again.

"Yeah, it was magic, Lenn," Simon said, smiling softly at her.

"I knew if I didn't come and talk to you, I'd regret it," Shannon said.

Lennox regained her composure as she took in all of our features. "It's very kind of you to offer, but we're currently doing SIT, a competition with LiveIt. I don't want to change my plans and leave these guys."

Shannon thought for a second, assessing the table. "Well, here's the thing. I have a good eye for talent, and I think if the band heard you, they'd want you to join the tour with them, and they might be a little more convincing than me."

"But I don't have any original songs. I just do covers. What could I bring to the tour? I'm no one." Her shoulders slumped.

"Many people start out doing covers, but the touring company has a group of writers that can help you find your voice. Not every day do I find someone with your pipes and stage presence." She stopped, thinking something over. "Where are you next?"

"Chattanooga," Simon answered.

Shannon's eyes lit up, a smile coming to her face. "I have a proposition. I can't tell you who the band is, but I can have them sit in on your next performance. They'll be close to Chattanooga in two days. Would that work?"

"Yes," I said, seeing the opportunity begin to grow before my eyes. Lennox looked at me, her eyes wide, but I could see the want there, the need to explore this. "Do you have a place in mind? We discovered the hard way that most places have a long list of performers."

"I know the perfect place. I'll get the band to show up, you sing, and then we'll take it from there. It also gives you a few days to think about the offer."

"What *is* the offer exactly?" I asked, feeling we needed all the details.

Shannon turned to me, a smile pulling at the corners of her lips. "And you are?"

"Thane Evans, boyfriend and manager." I held out my hand, taking hers.

"Ah, and that makes you two?" she asked, looking at Simon and Slade.

"Simon, boyfriend and stylist," Simon said with a wide grin. Slade rolled his eyes, sighing, but gave in to her questions since it was for Lennox.

"Boyfriend and bodyguard."

I held in a laugh at that, but I also knew he wasn't kidding. Shannon looked at us all in a new light, and I was thankful it wasn't a disgusted one.

"I think you'll have more in common with this band than you think," she muttered before turning back to me. "The touring company will provide lodging and meals and will give you a percentage of each ticket sold. You'll be responsible for negotiating that and royalties for songs that go viral."

"Thank you, and you'll let us know where to go in two days?"

"Absolutely." She handed me a business card. "Text me when you're in the city, and I'll give you the details." She turned back to Lennox. "It was wonderful to meet you, and I hope you'll consider the offer. I think you'll be a huge success. You've got that *it* factor." Shannon stood without another word, walking back to her table. We all stared at one another, unsure of what to do now.

"Did you just say you were my manager? And stylist? And you, my bodyguard?" Lennox asked, making us all laugh.

We finished our drinks, none of us talking about it yet, too afraid of bursting the magical bubble we seemed to be in with the offer. We listened to a few more people, but none of them seemed to have the same feel that Lennox had conjured while on stage. A few people came by, telling her how great she'd done, only making her blush more. But it was a good look on her.

"Should we head back? I know we want to see the ducks before we head out in the morning, so we need to be packed and ready before then," I said, looking around the table at my family.

"Yeah, I'm suddenly more eager to get to Chattanooga," Lennox said, smiling.

THE VAN WAS PACKED, and we were already checked out as we made our way to the Peabody Hotel. Lennox was bouncing on her toes as we stepped into the crowded lobby, jostling a few people to find good spots.

"Welcome, ladies and gentlemen," the Peabody duckmaster said, greeting everyone as he twirled a cane, and it landed on a rolled-up red carpet. He was decked out in a red coat and black pants, the only thing he was missing was a top hat, and he'd look like a circus ringmaster.

"Can I have your attention? Welcome to the historic Peabody Hotel and the famous fountain. Now, if I can direct your focus onto our guests of honor."

Just then, a speaker began to play a march as the ducks started to strut down the red carpet in single file. Lennox beamed next to me, clapping her hands. I had to admit, it was cute, even if a bit ridiculous.

They marched up little red-carpeted stairs and then got into formation around the fountain.

"I didn't know ducks could be that well trained," she whispered, leaning close.

"You can train just about most animals if you take the time," I said, watching the duckmaster as he paraded around with a lot of showmanship. I wondered if they had to audition for the role. It seemed pretty important as the three-minute spectacle drew a crowd every day.

Once they were all on their perches, everyone clapped, praising the ducks. Slade grunted, clearly not amused, but he couldn't deny the smile spreading across Lennox's face.

"You're not getting a duck," he said as she started to open her mouth.

"Good, I don't want one. I was going to ask if you've ever seen a duck penis before. It's shaped like a corkscrew." She humphed, turning on her heel, leaving Slade slack-jawed as she walked away.

Simon and I burst out laughing, following our mischievous girlfriend back out onto the street. Throwing my arm around her, I walked with her to a little bistro that had window service and we ordered coffee and chocolate croissants to go, munching as we returned to the van.

"Each new city we go to, I find something about it

to love. I don't think I could ever pick a favorite. Each one has something special about it. Babs was right, traveling with someone you love is the way to go," she sighed wistfully, leaning into me.

"My favorite is whichever you're in, Noxy girl." I kissed her head as we walked, knowing I meant every word.

I thought I was lost when I decided to take some time away from being a vet, but it turned out that my center had been right in front of me all along. Being with Lennox, Simon, and Slade made me feel at home and like I had a purpose. I loved animals, and helping them was something I would always want to do, but I didn't know if it was what I was meant to do for the rest of my life.

A new path was developing before me, and it was exciting to think of all the possibilities it could bring. Lennox hadn't mentioned anything more about the tour, but I could tell she was considering it. I'd jumped in, saying I was her manager so Shannon wouldn't think Lennox was unrepresented, but the more I tossed it around in my brain, the more at home it felt.

"I think I really do want to be your manager, Lennox," I blurted as we came around the bend, the van a few feet away.

Everyone stopped, looking at me. It had been

some weird unmentioned rule that we wouldn't bring up the tour until Lennox did, but I knew I needed to say something. In fact, I was bursting with energy over it.

"Really? Are you sure? I mean, I'm not even certain I want to do that. I love being a tattoo artist."

"Who says you can't be both, Peach?" Slade asked, lifting his eyebrow. "That's the great thing about tattoos. You can have a mobile office. Maybe our new shop doesn't need to be in a place, though I think I'll open one here. The energy is right for it. But perhaps we could do more things like this competition. Pop-up tattoos. Thane's been building a presence on LiveIt. We could use it to help us spread the word."

Lennox chewed on her lip as she debated. "But what about Simon? And is that doing too much? I don't want y'all to change your lives around for me."

Simon scoffed, walking forward to take her hand. "Lemon Drop, you're our whole world. I'm speaking for myself, but I'm sure the others agree. If I get to do a job where I also get to be with you, it's hands down the best job. This trip has been the best. You can't deny how amazing it's been to travel and see all these new things. The tour would be on a bigger scale. We'd get to see more places. This feels right. This is the opportunity we've been waiting for."

"What about the shops?" she asked. "You just opened Tattooed Hearts." Lennox looked at Slade.

"Bubba practically runs the BG store, and I can hire someone for the others. You can help me, so we don't have another… situation." He grimaced at the last word, but it did make Lennox think, considering what he was saying.

"So y'all would want to travel with me, even if it meant being crammed with people we didn't know for hours?"

"If anything, we can offer to drive our van if space is an issue, but I don't think it will be. This doesn't have to be forever, Noxy girl, but I think it's something you should do now. You never know if you'll get an opportunity like this again."

"How about you call your family and Darcie and talk it over with them, so it's not just our opinions?" Simon offered, making Lennox smile as she nodded.

"Deal. I can agree with that. So, I guess we should hit the road?"

We climbed into the van, our future still undecided, but I had a feeling it wouldn't stay that way for long.

Chapter Twenty

LENNOX

THE DRIVE to Chattanooga flew by, and before I knew it, we'd checked into another hotel. While each one had been amazing and a new experience, I was beginning to miss having more space. Maybe there was something to Slade's camping idea after all. It could be nice to get away from everything for a day.

Or perhaps that was just my way of saying I had no idea what I wanted.

A few years ago, heck, a few months ago, the idea of singing in front of a crowd on a regular basis scared the living daylights out of me.

But now… it felt kind of exciting. Okay, it felt exhilarating. And when Slade sang with me, it felt close to perfection.

The problem was that I didn't know if I could do it for more than one night. What if I was only suitable for karaoke or open mic? The thought of failing was paralyzing me. Which was odd. I didn't usually care.

Blowing out a breath, I stepped out onto the balcony, needing some air. My phone buzzed in my pocket, and I slid it out, glancing at the name.

Darcie.

Smiling, I instantly picked it up, knowing she'd set me straight.

"Hey, Darce! How are you?"

"Lennox, you'll never believe what just happened!"

Laughing, I listened to Darcie talk about a crazy dance Buck had her learn. There was some sadness in her voice, but I could tell she didn't want to talk about it. If I had to guess, the guy she'd been secretly seeing had called things off. Darcie had a dark past, and I knew when she was ready to tell me she would. So until then, I just reminded her how awesome she was and how much I appreciated her friendship.

"I can't wait to see this dance. Speaking of things you'll never believe, guess what I did?"

"Tattooed hottie Slade's initials on your boob? Got married? Got knocked up?" she gasped after each one, becoming more manic with her guesses.

"Holy pajamas! Darcie, you're ridiculous. I can't believe you go from tattoos to getting knocked up.

You're nuts, my friend." I giggled, wiping the tears from my eyes.

"Hey, I'm just saying. A little nugget that looked like your guys wouldn't be a bad thing."

"Anyways, I'm not pregnant. Not married. And the only tattoo I have is the one Slade gave me. But I did sing on stage, and a talent scout approached me."

"Shut up! Shut the front door! This is amazing, Lennox! What did you say? What did you do?"

"Well, they want me to sing tomorrow while we're here in Chattanooga. I haven't decided yet if I'm going to take the deal. It's a big decision."

"Um, no. It's an easy decision. Someone wants to give you a chance to share your gift with others and pay you to do it… winner, winner! What do the guys think?"

"Surprisingly, they're all on board. Zane said he was my manager, Simon my stylist, and Slade my bodyguard."

She broke out into laughter, making some of the tightness in my chest ease. "Oh, that's classic. Can I be your dance instructor? Please! I need to get out of Nashville." I could tell she was joking, but her voice also had some truth to it.

"What's going on? I thought you loved your job."

"Ugh, I do. It's just… not the same without you."

I knew that wasn't all the truth, but all she would give me for now.

"So you think I should say yes?"

"100%! This is an opportunity of a lifetime. Even if you never do anything else with music, you can't deny that this would be a great experience. You love to sing, and if you got to do it for a while, you might not find it as scary. Think of the stories you can tell your grandkids when you're old."

"You know, since we've been on this convention competition thing, it hasn't felt as scary," I admitted.

"So maybe you just needed to spread your wings a little all along."

"Yeah, you could be right." I sighed, smiling.

"I love it when you say that. Say it again!"

"Darcie is right."

"Damn straight. All joking aside. I miss you, but I think you should do this. What would *you* say if I was calling and saying that someone offered me this opportunity?"

"Were they deaf? Because you can't sing."

"Har-de-har-har. Fine. If it was for dancing, what then, smart ass?"

Laughing, I chewed on my lip, knowing what she meant. "I'd tell you to take it and don't even second guess it."

"Exactly. It's a tour. Not a life commitment.

Either you love or hate it, but either way, you'll know you tried, and I think that's what you need the most."

"Yeah. Okay. I'll hear what they have to say."

"My job here is done. Now, go and be awesome, and hurry back."

"Yes, ma'am. We should be back in less than a week. We have a few more days before we're on our way back to Bowling Green. It's been fun, but boy, do I miss my bed."

"Sweet. Let's plan something when you're back. I need some girl time."

Again, I could hear the despair, and I knew I'd need to take her up on that and make sure to plan something.

"Absolutely. Love you, Darce. Thanks for being awesome."

"Back at ya, Lennox. Kisses."

We hung up, and I had to agree I felt lighter after talking with her. I stared out over the city, breathing the air in deep, excited about what tomorrow would bring.

The door opened, and I turned, spotting Slade. "You ready to go to the aquarium?"

Nodding, I walked forward, taking his hand. He didn't move, staring down at me, assessing every detail.

"You decided," he said after a few moments passed.

"How do you do that?" I asked, not denying it.

"It's in your eyes. You seem more assured than when you stepped out here."

Circling my arms around his waist, I leaned against his hard abs and pecs. "I love how much you notice things. I always thought you were calculating all the ways you hated me, but it wasn't that."

"No, I was trying to commit to memory every detail because I never thought I'd have you."

Tears wanted to surface at what we almost lost, but I pushed them down. They didn't belong here. Darcie was right in that I didn't need to question the things in my life, but to take hold of them and conquer whatever fears I had. It helped when I had three amazing men to do it with.

"Let's go see some fish," I said, kissing his chest before I stepped back.

"What are the odds we leave without you wanting to take something home?" Slade asked as we stepped into the room. My eyes met Zane's, and we both laughed, shrugging.

"Fucking hell." Slade dropped his head back, letting out a long breath before he zeroed in on Zane and me. "Fine. You can have a goat. But that's it."

He stomped out of the room, grabbing Simon's

hand as he did, leaving a shock-faced Zane and me behind. Once the door shut, we both succumbed to our giggles, barely able to stop them before we made it out into the hall.

"Yes!" I whispered as we walked to the elevator. "What should we name our goat?"

"Billy is too obvious," Zane said, thinking about it.

"True. We'll have to wait for the perfect name to come."

Slade gave us a look when we neared, but I caught the barest hint of a smile as we stepped into the elevator, and I wondered just how much he was pretending to not want a goat.

We caught a car service to the aquarium, not wanting to deal with parking. Stepping into the building, I was already in awe at the beautiful fish display.

"This place has over 12,000 fish and 800 species," I said, reading from the brochure. Slade grabbed my hand, pulling me along as we started to make our way through. Seeing all the fish was magical, and I knew if he wasn't dragging me, I would've stayed looking at one section for hours.

"Come on, I want to see the Ocean Journey," Slade said, urging me through the River Journey portion.

"Fine, but only because there are penguins."

Slade snorted, but didn't stop until we came to the Secret Reef. He stood, watching the sharks and stingrays swim, transfixed by them. It was a whole new side that had me observing him more than the fish for once.

He glanced over, finding me watching him as his cheeks heated. "What?"

"I just never took you for a shark enthusiast. It's cute."

"Sharks are awesome," he scoffed, like that was the only thing that mattered.

Pulling his arm around me, I snuggled in close as we watched the fish swimming, utterly ignorant of us. It was peaceful, and I relaxed as we stood there.

Simon and Zane caught up to us, standing with us as we watched. After a while, it felt like I could say my deepest dreams here, and it would matter. That observing the Secret Reef made me brave enough to share my own secrets.

"I want to do the tour. If you guys will go with me. I mean, if they ask us and the band isn't an awful one."

They all looked at me, smiling, and my shoulders dropped, the last of the tension leaving my body.

"They'd be stupid not to want you, Lenn. Sounds like our next adventure is calling us."

As we walked through the rest of the aquarium, stopping to see the penguins on their rock, some jellyfish and art, and even butterflies, I felt lighter and not so out of place for once.

Buying a few postcards and pins for my collection, we headed out a few hours later, discussing where to grab some dinner. Which, of course, meant we had to run into Lee.

"Well, well, well…" he sneered, taking in our group.

"I'm starting to think you're my new stalker," I said, rolling my eyes. Slade growled, sending a different feeling to my lady bits. Hot mama alert!

"You wish." He laughed, which was not the right move for him.

The three men who'd been mostly ignoring him for over a week stiffened, their stances changing as they took in the man who'd decided today was a good day to diss me.

"Oh man, wrong choice of words there."

Lee, for once gulped, realizing the danger he might be in. Only the crowd around us was saving him from having his ugly face bashed in.

"How about you leave us alone and leave the trash talking to tattoos, asswipe?" Slade said, practically spitting at the man. "We have no problem with you. You're the one who keeps seeking us out. Stay in your lane, and we won't have any issues. Understood?"

"Yeah, man, sorry. I got carried away. No disrespect. I'll stay away. Um, good luck."

Lee ran away so fast that I wondered if I'd imagined the whole ordeal. Once he was gone, the guys calmed down before breaking out into laughter.

"Did you see his face? I think he was this close to pissing himself."

Walking down the street, we found a restaurant without a line and took our seats, the guys praising one another for their excellent scare tactics on Lee. I didn't mention how I'd handled him all the previous times. They could have this win. I was just glad it hadn't resulted in punches. Maybe tomorrow we could get through the competition without more visits from Lee.

No matter what, I knew it would be a hard day to concentrate, with the audition looming afterward. It didn't scare me, though. In fact, I was feeling more invigorated than I ever had before.

It was time for this songbird to spread her wings and sing.

Chapter Twenty-One

LENNOX

THE MORNING HAD FLOWN BY, and I was finalizing my sketch of a woodland scene at our booth. Simon had already started his hair and makeup, so it was just Slade and me for the moment. So far, Lee had stayed true to his word, and we hadn't heard a peep from him. Just a few side-eyed looks when he didn't think anyone was looking.

"I can't believe I'm saying this, but I'm ready to return to Kentucky," Slade said, stretching. "I'm getting too old to bed hop."

Snorting, I looked up at him, taking in all the tattoos on his neck. "Yeah? How's a bus going to be any better?" I bit my lip as I waited for him to say something.

"Nah. It will be fine. I'm just moaning."

"You?" I gasped, giggling.

"What?" he asked, narrowing his eyes at me. "I don't complain regularly."

"Yeah, okay."

Snickering, I shaded in one more area, finishing the last spot. It was one of the more detailed tattoos I'd done, but it wasn't bringing the same sense of exhilaration I'd grown accustomed to. I turned it to Slade so he could see it.

"What do you think?"

"It's good. Real good. You're getting better each time, Peach." I smiled, turning it back. The compliment felt nice, but for some reason, it didn't feel like it should.

"What is it?" he asked, pulling me closer.

"I don't know. I think I'm just nervous about tonight, so my mind's a little preoccupied."

He looked around quickly, taking in the crowd and time. "I have an idea." Slade grabbed my hand and tugged me up, pulling me down a row and then behind some dividers. He kept walking; the crowd separated by blue partitions. The noise was slightly muted, but you could still hear people as they mingled and talked with competitors.

"Where are we going?" I squeaked when Slade kept towing me along.

"Somewhere I can distract your mind." He

winked at me, a devilish smile on his face that instantly heated up my lady parts. When he came to another section a few feet down, he moved around some of the dividers that had created a little room.

"How did you know this was here?" I asked.

"It's my business to know the layout."

He shrugged like that answered the question. Before I could ask him another one, he lifted me up and sat me on some old speakers, bringing me more to his height.

"Um, hi," I said, feeling shy suddenly, my cheeks heating.

Slade ran his fingers through my hair, watching as the pink and green strands fell over his hand. "It's time I see if you taste like watermelon sugar."

His inked fingers pushed up my skirt, baring my quickly dampening panties to him. Slade spread my legs wider as he bent down to rub his nose up the middle. My thighs began to tremble from the promise of what was to come. Leaning back on my hands, I offered myself up to Slade, ready for whatever he had in store.

Slade pulled my panties to the side, teasing me with his tongue as it peeked out and touched my clit. My body moved, rocking toward him as it sought more. Slade's laugh rumbled against my thigh, sending vibrations through me, causing a whimper to leave my lips.

"There are still people close by, Peach. You gotta be quiet."

I nodded, not able to use words, too afraid I'd let something escape if I opened my mouth. Squeezing my eyes shut tight, I didn't see how he managed to slip my panties off, but the next second, his mouth was entirely on me, and I fell back to my elbows, my thighs going to his shoulders as he began to devour me.

His tongue swept up slowly before he sucked on my clit. As he lavished attention on my button, he began to drag his fingers in and out at such a slow pace I was a writhing mess. A whimper left me as I tried to pull him toward me, needing more.

"Fuck, Peach. I'd only meant to drive you to an orgasm, but the way you're wiggling on my fingers, clamping down around them like you want more, has me harder than glass. Slide down, Peach."

In a daze, I barely caught what he wanted as I slid off the speaker, and he turned me, bracing my elbows on it. My skirt was still over my waist, the cold air kissing my butt cheeks. Before I could ask him what was going on, he dragged me back toward him, his cock brushing against my center a second before he slammed into me.

The force pushed me against the speaker, and I tucked my head into my arms, hoping to muffle some of my cries of pleasure. Slade didn't waste any time, feeling the need as urgently as I. He breathed into my neck, muffling his own moans.

"Your pussy is sweeter than ever, Peach. I couldn't just have a taste. I needed the whole thing. Hold on, this is going to be quick."

Slade's hand moved around to my front, and he dragged some lubrication and began to circle my clit as he thrust in and out, hitting me deep. My legs began to tremble, and I tensed around him as my orgasm began to build. Reaching across the speaker, I gripped the other side as my head fell back onto his shoulder, and I braced myself for him to send me over.

With a few more deep thrusts, Slade's cock hit me just right, and I fell apart around him as I muffled my screams into his neck, biting down when I couldn't hold it in anymore. The little bit of pain had Slade falling apart in me as his knees buckled, and we almost face-planted into the speaker.

Laughing, he caught us, drawing us together as he slowly slipped out of me. Kissing me deeply, he gently brushed my hair before taking my hand and leading me back out to the crowd. I spotted a bathroom a few feet away and pointed to it.

Nodding, we both headed into our respective ones to clean up. Using the bathroom quickly, I attempted to freshen up so I wouldn't smell of sex while I was tattooing someone. Washing my hands, I dried them and then fixed my hair, smoothing down some flyaways. Satisfied, I walked out, finding Slade waiting for me.

"Do I get my panties back?" I whispered.

"Nope." He smirked, taking my hand, and I rolled my eyes. He thought he was cute, but fortunately, I had a plan in mind. No way was I going to try to tattoo a stranger without anything on underneath.

When we got back to the booth, I glanced around, something feeling off, but I shook it off and grabbed my purse.

"I'll be right back."

I winked this time as someone approached Slade, effectively trapping him at the booth. He gave me a look to get back there, but I just waved. I wasn't going far, and it was a public place. What was the worst that could happen?

Thankfully, there wasn't a line at the booth I'd been eyeing for the past three cities. It was a booty short booth that printed a design on the butt cheeks of them in the shop. They looked super soft and comfortable. A woman was wearing a pair as she heat-pressed the orders, and two guys wore the male version. I was half tempted to buy the guys some, but I didn't know if they'd actually wear them.

"What can we get you, sweetheart?"

"Thick thighs, witchy vibes," I said, pointing to a purple pair. He smiled, grabbing them and showing me the size. I was impressed when he'd guess right.

"Yep. You're good at that."

He winked, handing them to the girl and telling her which design. While she pressed them, he took my payment, asking me what I was here for.

"I'm part of the tattoo competition."

"Really, that's cool. Which booth?"

I turned and pointed to ours. "Tattooed Hearts. See that scary dude? That's one of my boyfriends. He's mad I left him to deal with the people," I teased.

The guy laughed, nodding at Slade. "I'll have to stop by and check out your stuff later." He handed me the bag, and I noticed how he was respectful and didn't try to cop a feel.

"Thanks. I can't wait to wear them. And please stop by."

He smiled, nodding, going to the next customer. I managed to find another bathroom and pulled the booty shorts on. I was glad they'd been sealed beforehand, though I was almost desperate enough to wear them even if they hadn't been. I pulled up the hip-hugging shorts and instantly knew I needed more.

"Oh man, these are amazing." Shoving my skirt down, I made a mental note to look at more of their designs when I walked by because I needed more. Maybe I'd get Simon some of the guys kind. He'd be totally down for it.

When I walked back to the booth, the announcer was going over the contest rules and stating how this was the end of the first leg of the competition. He briefly ran through the rankings, and I was surprised when we were in third. I hadn't been paying much attention to the standings since we were just doing this for fun.

Slade eyed me as I skirted around the table, grabbing my design to verify with the client, but thankfully, he was busy with his own, so he couldn't ask me anything.

Printing it out, I began to set up my table when I realized what was wrong. I looked under the booth, behind it, and on Slade's, but all of my ink was gone.

"Fiddlesticks!"

"What?" Slade asked, stopping what he was doing.

"My ink is gone. Someone took it."

Slade's nostrils flared, and he glanced over at Lee, who did everything in his power to keep his gaze off us. A LiveIt official walked up, noticing that we hadn't started.

"Everything alright?"

"Someone tampered with my ink. It's gone."

She eyed the stand and looked back at me. "You can't leave the area once the timer starts, so I'm afraid you'll have to withdraw from today's competition."

My heart sank, my head dropping as I tried to hold back the tears. My recklessness would cost me this time.

"She can use mine," Slade said, stopping the official from doing whatever she was about to. "I'll withdraw if I need to in her place."

I looked up, shaking my head that he didn't have to, even though I knew he would do what he wanted. Zane and Simon walked up as we started to argue about who would continue.

"What's going on?" Simon asked.

"I'm withdrawing. Lennox, get started. You need all of your time," Slade said, leaving no room for argument. He pushed his cart over, unscrewing my gun and putting the ink pot on mine. Sighing, I knew there was no stopping him at this point.

Sitting down, I smiled weakly at the client as I placed the tattoo transfer on her thigh. Simon walked up behind me, massaging my shoulders. He put my earbuds in my ears a few seconds later, and I took a deep breath, trying to block out all the outside. I felt this was Lee's doing, but we couldn't prove it, and dwelling on it now wouldn't help.

With the assistance of some good music, I fell into my groove, blocking out the world as I began my tattoo.

When I looked up a few hours later, I wiped the sweat from my brow as I glanced around, looking for the clock. A sigh left me as I realized I'd made it. I had five minutes left. Standing, I stretched my neck and fingers as an official took a picture. It looked like I was the last one, but it was done, and that was all that mattered after the rough start.

"I love it," the girl said. I couldn't remember her name; too many other things on my mind this time.

"I'm glad. It's beautiful." She beamed at me, listening as Slade went over the aftercare for me. I slumped down into Simon's arms, letting him hold me. I was beat, and the thought of singing tonight no longer felt exciting.

"I'm so tired of people trying to steal something from me," I whispered, a tear falling. I wiped it away, not wanting them to see it.

"I know you are, Lenn. But no matter how much they try, they never succeed. People always want to steal your sunshine because you shine so bright. You do it so effortlessly that they don't understand it, so they try to take it. You can't give up your dream. Not now. So take a moment to recharge, but find that fire that is all you, and rally. We'll be right here when you're ready."

He kissed my forehead, and I knew he was right. This was just a blip, but it didn't have to be how the story ended. Closing my eyes, I breathed in Simon's scent, letting it center me as I relaxed in his arms.

"Sorry to bother you, but I just wanted to say what an awesome portfolio you have." I opened my eyes, the guy from the booty-short booth standing across from me. Sitting up, I smoothed down my clothes as I processed what he said.

"Oh, thank you. I need to come and get some more of these shorts because they are amazing. I'm hoping I can convince this one to try them too."

The guy glanced at Simon, curiosity in his gaze, but he didn't say anything about this not being the same guy I told him was my boyfriend earlier.

"I might have a proposition for you then. What would you say about teaming up?"

I sat up straighter, instantly intrigued. "Go on… what do you mean?"

"Well, we're always looking for people to create new designs. What if we created a Tattooed Hearts line? Of course, you'd get unlimited booty shorts for your own personal use."

"Yes, sold." I laughed, knowing I probably needed more details. But the man had just offered me free underwear. He could call them booty shorts all he wanted, but they were underwear. Really comfortable underwear.

He smiled, his shoulders relaxing. He started to talk when the announcer came on again.

"I'll take care of the details for you, Noxy girl. Go and show Inkjection we don't bow to bullies," Zane said, stepping up to the guy.

"Inkjection? That guy is a tool." He rolled his eyes.

"I'm Lennox, by the way, and I like you even more for your taste in humans."

"I'm Ethan." He stuck his hand out, and I shook it before turning to Zane.

"This is Zane; he'll get the details. I look forward to working with you, Ethan."

I jumped up, tugging Simon with me as we headed to the podium so we could hear the scores. Slade was waiting for us, lifting his eyebrow when I walked up.

"Who was that guy?" he asked.

"Someone who thinks Lee and InkJection is a tool

and offered Lennox a job designing underwear," Simon said, smiling at Slade.

"Humph," he said, having nothing to say to that. "Well, okay."

Laughing, I shook my head. Simon won another award but didn't place high enough to win grand prizes. He was still happy with the award he won and said that he'd learned a lot and had made some good networking connections, so that was what really mattered.

"Our final award is a tie," the announcer said. "Inkjection and Tattooed Hearts both showed ingenuity and creativity in their designs today."

Both of our tattoos were displayed on the screen, and it was cool seeing mine up there, even if I did have to share it. I walked up, ignoring Lee as I accepted the award.

"Which brings us to the overall scores for the first portion of our competition. Our runner-up is Tattooed Hearts with Inkjection taking overall winner."

Slade growled next to me. If we'd both had entered today, we probably would've secured it, but I realized as I walked up there that it didn't matter. We knew our tattoos were good. We didn't need a score or award to confirm that. Besides, at the end of the day, we didn't have to sabotage others to ensure we won. Living a life of joy was more my speed.

Again, I ignored Lee, smiling as I took the award. The only people I focused on were my three guys, who stood together, looking at me like they were the real winners.

Besides, I'd just been given an unlimited supply of booty-shorts. I bet Lee couldn't claim that.

Chapter Twenty-Two

LENNOX

SHAKING OUT MY HANDS, I took a few deep breaths as I tried to slow my heart. The bar was loud behind me, but I focused on the songs I was about to sing, going over the choices in my head.

After the competition, we returned to the hotel and rested for a bit before meeting our mystery group. Shannon had messaged Zane that she'd gotten me a three-song time spot at Sing it or Wing it, one of the popular karaoke bars in the area. The guys were excited to try some of the wings, but I was too nervous to eat.

"Noxy girl, you're going to smash it," Zane whispered, taking my hands. Looking up, I nodded as I tried to relax.

"I don't know why I'm so nervous," I admitted.

His eyes softened, and he pulled me into his arms. I went willingly, his aftershave wafting over me and instantly calming my heart. Zane held me tight, kissing my hair as he did. I should've done this sooner.

"Don't think about anything other than just going out there and singing. You do your best when you're not worried and just have fun. That's what this is all about. Okay?"

Nodding, I stepped back, giving him a wobbly smile. "Yeah, you're right."

The stage manager poked her head around, giving me the nod that it was time. Zane kissed me on the cheek, and I took one final breath as I stepped up to the microphone. The crowd cheered as I took it, and I smiled at them.

"Good evening, folks. I'm Lennox James, and I'll start tonight with 'Ugly' by Ella Henderson. I hope you like it."

The music started, and I closed my eyes as the first words crossed my lips. *"Too thin, too smart. Monday, don't fit in my jeans, stretch marks."*

My voice filled the room unlike it had ever before. I sank into the words, putting everything I felt into them. When I first heard the song, it had resonated with me, making me realize I wasn't the only girl to ever feel that way, and singing about it gave me a voice so that others knew it too. Or, at least that was what I hoped.

"It's okay to be lost, to feel lonely. Sometimes I just don't know what I'm doing. One day I'm beautiful, then I'm ugly, but those days, they remind me that I'm human."

As the song continued, I felt myself growing more confident, the words becoming my anthem, making me embrace everything I was singing. By the end, my eyes were open, and I felt the music in my bones, doing a little shimmy. When the song ended, it was quiet for a second before applause exploded, and I laughed, tears hitting my eyes. It had been right to sing that song here, to feel the crowd's acceptance at the end of this journey, no matter what else came of it.

"Thank you. Wow, that was quite the applause. For my next song, I'll need my boyfriend to help me. He might need some convincing, though. You guys want to help?" I smiled, winking at Slade. He rolled his eyes but walked over to the side of the stage as the crowd started shouting for him to join me.

"Join her, join her."

I'd given him the heads up that I might ask, so he'd borrowed a guitar and had tuned it. I knew if I told him I wanted him to sing, he would've tried to talk me out of it, so I made it sound like I was still debating songs when I'd already picked to sing this with him.

"Now, this song is very popular at the moment on the country charts and a perfect duet. Here's our rendition of 'Never Say Never' by Cole Swindell and Lainey Wilson."

As we started to sing back and forth, trading the lyrics, I was ensnared in his eyes. While the lyrics didn't fit us as a couple anymore, it reminded me of not long ago when we were in that back and forth pull with one another. One thing was certain, I would never say never with Slade Evans. He was one of the loves of my life, and I wanted to spend every moment I could with him. Forever.

"You're all I want, I'll never say never with you."

Slade's eyes held mine the whole time, and it felt like we were the only people in the room as we sang to one another. One thing had been made clear to me no matter what transpired tonight. I needed to do this—sing. Most importantly, I needed to sing with him.

The song ended, and he didn't waste time, pulling me into a heated kiss. The crowd cheered as they hooted, making my cheeks blush. Slade leaned down into the microphone, addressing the people.

"Just so we're clear, I'll always say yes to her. Don't anyone go and get any ideas." He said it with a rumble in his voice, making goosebumps appear on my skin. Rolling my eyes, I pushed him off the stage, feeling the high of performing, taking over.

"Okay, wow, singing with him is always a treat." I fanned my face as everyone laughed, giving me a few seconds to catch my breath. "For my last song, I decided to leave you with a little upbeat number. For the past two weeks, I've been traveling from city to city with my boyfriends. Yes, plural. What's been amazing about this trip is meeting new people and seeing new adventures. Before this, I hadn't been more than an hour from my hometown. So, to say it has been eye-opening is an understatement. This song, I feel, represents this trip for me. 'Moments We Live For' by In Paradise."

I began to sing, the tune of the music filling my body as I tapped my foot along to it, swishing my hips. When I got to the chorus, it burst out of me as I was practically vibrating.

"These are the moments, the moments we live for."

I spread my arms wide, finding my guys in the crowd watching me with pure love on their faces. I twirled around, my watermelon hair swinging out behind me. A year ago, I felt stuck in the same routine, wishing and wanting more in my life. I never imagined it possible that a stalker would lead me to three men who owned my heart, a job I loved, and a passion for singing again. Babs had been right about getting out and experiencing life. There was so much out there, and I just had to take the chance. Nothing was guaranteed, but never trying meant not singing in a karaoke bar in Chattanooga, Tennessee.

That felt like the worst possible outcome at the moment—to have never experienced this.

Finishing the song, I held the last note for an extra second, a tear of happiness filling my eye as I realized I'd done it. I'd sung my heart out. The applause was deafening as everyone clapped and screamed, filling me up in a way I'd never thought possible. I wanted this. Now, I just had to make it happen.

"Thank you. Y'all have been great. I'm Lennox James, and I'm out!" I blew kisses, waving as I walked off the stage. A few people were waiting to tell me how good of a job I'd done. I nodded, but my attention was on the three guys off to the side. Once I was clear of the crowd, I ran, needing to feel their arms wrapped around me.

They pulled me into them instantly, and I sank into the feeling of them, knowing my life would be amazing because they were in it.

"I love you guys."

"We love you, Lenn," Simon said, kissing my

head. Slade grunted like it was obvious, but I felt his hand tighten around me, steadying me.

"There's someone here to talk with you, Lennox," Zane said as we pulled apart. "You'll never believe who it is."

He took my hand and led me to the back corner that was dimly lit. Several guys and a girl were sitting there. At first, I didn't recognize who it was as the beautiful redhead and the giant blonde guy took up the end, but I realized as I looked further that it was on purpose.

I stopped, my mouth dropping open as I realized that sitting a few feet from me was Shadows of Mayhem.

"You're Aspen, you're Jett, and you're Zion." I looked around, pointing them out like an idiot. When I got to the end, there was another guy I didn't know. "Where's Roscoe?" I asked as they all watched me, grins on most of their faces.

"Hey babe, you do have fans," the redhead said, nudging her shoulder into Aspen. He threw his head back, letting out a loud uproarious laugh, and I stumbled forward more as Zane pushed me. Jett smirked at me, looking me over, but then went back to talking to Zion.

"Sorry, when I first met Penny, she wasn't impressed at all by me being in a band," Aspen said, reaching out across the table to shake my hand. "It's nice to meet you, Lennox."

I shook his hand, looking at everyone. "Wait, I know you as well. You're part of LiveIt's reality show. You're the DIY girl. Wow. I think I'm going to faint."

Penny blushed, but nodded. "Wow, it's still weird to have people know me."

"Have a seat, Peach," Slade said, pushing a chair under me. He sat beside me, spreading his legs wide as he took in the group. I glanced back at the band, not sure what to say. Thankfully, Zane was there to lead the way.

"Shannon said that you might be interested in having Lennox join you?" he asked, sitting next to me. I glanced over, finding that Simon was sitting on Slade's other side.

"Yes, actually. She sent us a video of you singing one of our songs," Jett said, searing me with his eyes. The man had a magnetism that made me hot around the collar. Slade scooted closer to me, grunting as he placed his arm around me.

"Oh, I hope I didn't embarrass myself." My cheeks heated, and I began to fiddle with my hands.

"On the contrary. We loved what you did with it. You have an amazing voice, and it's magic when you and Slade sing together," Aspen said, smiling warmly at me.

I looked up at my surly boyfriend, grinning at him. He watched me, ignoring the others. I glanced back, finding Penny observing me, a soft smile on her face.

"I agree. He's not one for singing a lot, though. So, what are you suggesting, exactly?"

"Well, our opening act had to back out of this new tour we're about to start. There was an issue with Roscoe and their lead singer, so not only are we looking for a new opener, but we just auditioned new drummers."

"Oh wow, that's stressful."

"Tell me about it," Jett sighed, wiping his face.

"Shannon said you don't have a lot of original material, but you could sing some songs with us. I've been playing around with adding female vocals, and I think your voice would pair well with Jett's," Aspen said. I felt Slade's arm tighten on the chair, but I ignored him. "I've also been writing some new original songs and working with another songwriter on things that are a little different from our brand that I think would be perfect for your range. We can discuss all of that if you're interested."

I looked at my guys, knowing I couldn't make

this without them. "Well, it's not just me. These three are kind of a package deal."

"So Shannon said. I believe you're the manager," Aspen said, looking to Zane, "the stylist," to Simon, and "the bodyguard?" to Slade.

Giggling, I patted Slade's leg. "Something like that."

"Well, it so happens that we're also in an untraditional relationship," Aspen said, pointing at himself, Penny, the blonde guy, and the other dark-haired guy. "So, we understand unique situations."

I looked at them with a new understanding. Penny had a carefree spirit about her, making me instantly like her.

"It would be nice to have another female on tour," she whispered. "Especially one who also has three boyfriends. Perhaps we could trade tips." She giggled, and I smiled, nodding.

"Just so we're clear on the terms," Zane began, "she opens for you and occasionally might sing with you. You'll help her find some original songs."

"Sounds about right. The rest of the stuff you'll iron out with the tour company. But yes, we'd love for you to join us if you're interested. We have to go and meet our new drummer, Griffin, or we'd hang out longer. We'll be here until tomorrow, and then we're heading to practice for a week before the tour starts."

"Oh wow, that's soon." I swallowed, nerves beginning to envelop me. "What if I get stage fright?" I asked.

"You're a natural. You'll be fine once you get out there," Aspen said, making me believe it.

"Here's my number. Text or call when you decide, and we'll get things squared away with the Songbird," the dark-haired guy said. "I'm Rafe, and the blonde is Cooper," he said when I looked at him with a question.

"Simon, Slade, Zane, I mean Thane," I said, pointing at the guys in order.

Zane reached his hand out, taking the card. "We'll be in touch." We stood so they could get out, shaking hands as they passed. Penny pulled me into a hug, surprising me.

"I think we'll be great friends."

They walked off, and I felt like some of the brightness of the club left with them. I'd never met a famous band before, and they definitely had that star power about them.

I looked at the guys, smiling. "I can't believe I could be going on tour with Shadows of Mayhem. Someone pinch me. I feel like I'm dreaming."

"You're not dreaming, Peach. Come on. Let's go back to the room. We have something to celebrate."

My cheeks heated, and I took his hand as we left the bar. All I could think about the whole way to the hotel was how true my last song had been. These were the moments.

Chapter Twenty-Three

LENNOX

IT FELT bittersweet to be headed home after being on the road for two weeks. Of course, I was excited to head home, see my family, and tell them about the new opportunity. We'd have a week at home before we'd need to leave, but that felt like a lifetime when I was excited about our next adventure. The sound of the trunk shutting made me glance at all the guys.

"Well, that's it. Our open road adventure is done," I said, smiling at them. "One last, to Babs!" I shouted. The guys laughed, joining in.

"I think we have time for one more detour," Slade said, grinning widely at me, "but it's a surprise."

My three boyfriends stared at me as I tried to decipher the message. Shrugging my shoulders because I trusted them, I climbed into the van. It was quiet as Slade backed out and began driving, the music wasn't even on. I guess we were all comfortable with our own thoughts.

Pulling out my notebook, I began to sketch some designs for the booty shorts to occupy myself. We'd woken up to a gift basket this morning filled with several more pairs in my size and even some guy shorts for all three of my boyfriends. Ethan was a freaking wizard at guessing sizes.

As the pen moved across the page, I recalled all the crazy things that'd happened yesterday, from having sex in semi-public, having my ink tampered with, scoring a designing gig and free underwear, and singing like it was the most natural thing to do. And, of course, it still felt like a dream meeting Shadows of Mayhem.

Simon nudged my arm, and I glanced up, finding him watching me. "I know this is a rhetorical question, but are you excited? S.O.M is an amazing band."

I grinned, nodding. "I was just thinking how unreal it felt. You know, last night when I was on stage, I kind of had an epiphany. Even before we met the band, I was thankful our journey had led us right where we were. Last August, I'd been stuck, too scared to do anything and feeling like I would never meet anyone. Stalker aside, I happen to love the journey we've taken. From living on my own in

Nashville, to finally starting to do tattoos, to moving in with my three boyfriends, it's all been amazing."

"I thought I had my whole life mapped out. Work at the salon, pine after you and Slade, and live with my best friend for the rest of my life. Though I must admit, it was becoming much harder to live with you and not touch you, feel you, kiss you." He moved closer, brushing his lips across my chin, proving that he could now. "I'm so glad I don't have to stop myself anymore." Tilting my chin up, he placed a soft kiss on my lips with enough heat to zing me right to my core.

"Me too," I breathed, smiling into the kiss. "I'm glad you're all crazy enough to go with me on this. I don't think I would do it without you. Now that we're an us, I want us to be together. That's probably not how it's supposed to work, but I'm not going to question it for the time being."

Simon chuckled, draping his arm around my shoulders as I continued to draw. It wasn't long before we pulled up to a restaurant. The sign read Taqueria Paisanos. I blinked, not understanding why we'd come here.

"Where are we?" I asked, glancing around. It looked like a small town similar to Bowling Green.

"Dalton, Georgia. I figured we'd put one more state on your adventure and get some tasty tacos.

Plus, it was on the list to go to five states and do something only locals know. A few girls commented on our LiveIt posts that we should check out this place before we headed home. Besides, you're wearing your taco dress. It seemed like a sign."

I glanced down, like I'd forgotten what I'd been wearing, and realized he was right. Tacos were life. Giggling, I climbed out of the van, excited about trying some. We walked into the restaurant, the air conditioning bringing goosebumps to my skin as we headed to a table. After reviewing the menu, we placed our order and looked at one another.

"What?" I asked when no one said anything. Zane laughed, pushing a piece of hair back.

"You just seem happier and free. I'm glad you're doing this, Noxy girl."

"I don't like that guy," Slade added, grunting. "If anyone is going to sing with you, it's me."

Rolling my eyes, I smiled. "I love you, Tatzilla. If I sing with someone else, that's not going to change. I'd love to sing with you, though. Any time."

Slade took a chip, biting into it, not liking that I wouldn't refuse to sing with someone else. Part of me liked the idea of him being possessive and what that might bring after a show if I sang with Jett. The vision of how he might manhandle me some more had me squeezing my legs together as I shifted in my seat. Thankfully, I was saved by some tacos before I embarrassed myself.

"Oh my heavens," I moaned, taking a bite. "This is delicious." The guys all nodded, too consumed with their food to say anything else.

In quick succession, we all finished our tacos, and I already wished we had more. Slade got up to pay for it as we cleaned up our table. The door jangled as we began to walk toward it, and two girls walked in. They stopped instantly, looking at me, their mouths hanging open.

"You're Lennox. You're Simon," they said, pointing at us.

I stopped, stunned that someone outside of Bowling Green knew my name. "Um, hi. Do we know you?" I asked.

"Sorry, big fans. We follow you on LiveIt and came and saw you yesterday. We didn't get picked for either of you, but it was still fun to watch," one of them said as she smiled at us. "I'm Emily, and this is Megan." She pointed to her friend, who was still staring, her mouth wide as Slade caught up to us.

"Hubba hubba," she said when he placed his arm around Simon, and I was almost certain I was about to see someone faint, fangirl style.

Her friend nudged her, and they walked over to the counter as we made our way to the door. I turned, waving as we walked out, still unsure of what had just happened. Slade gave me a look, and I shook my head.

Yeah, Megan. I got it. He made me speechless sometimes too.

We climbed back into the van, settling in with our full tummies as we set off for home.

Thanks for one hell of a trip, Babs.

AFTER ONE PIT STOP, we pulled up to our driveway four hours later. It was odd coming home for once. I was happy to be here, but everything felt different. It didn't quite feel like it fit anymore.

Climbing out of the van, I stretched, twisting side-to-side as I took a deep breath of home. A horn honked behind us, and I turned to find my family pulling up. Instantly, I took off, running to them.

My little brother was out of the car first, much to my parent's disappointment, as he flung his arms around me.

"Oh my goodness, you've grown a foot taller!" I hugged him back, glad he wasn't too old to give me hugs. I pulled away, messing with his hair as I inspected him. "Hey, kiddo. I missed you. So much that I brought you a gift."

"Yes!" he shouted, stepping back to hug the guys while I gave my parents theirs.

"Hey, pumpkin," my dad said, squeezing me tight. He kissed my forehead, moving so my mom could get hers.

"Hey, Mom, Dad." My mother wiped her eyes, smiling at me. When I went to ask her what it was about, she shook her head, clearly not wanting to talk about it.

"How was the last part of your trip? Tell us everything," she said, walking me into the house as the guys began to unload the van.

After getting everything unloaded, ordering some pizza, and handing out the souvenirs I'd brought for my family, I updated them on the last day and everything that went down.

"Wow, so many awesome things. I can't wait to try these underwear if they're as soft as you say," my mom said.

"I can't wait to go back to school and tell all my friends that my sister is a rockstar!" Noah shouted, eating his fifth piece of salt water taffy.

"More like rockstar adjacent. I'll just be there. Not famous."

"Yet," Simon teased. "You had some fans today."

"So did you." I stuck out my tongue, his cheeks heating.

Once the last of the pizza was finished, I wished my parents goodbye, and sorted all the clothes for washing, ready to relax and be home.

Shoving the next load into the washer, I started it and made my way into the living room, where I found all three guys lounging in nothing but the boy booty shorts.

Stopping in my tracks, I stared from one to the other. The boys' shorts were longer than the girl's, but they were shorter than most of the shorts I'd seen my guys in. Not to mention how body-hugging they were wrapped around their thighs like a koala.

"You got some drool," Simon said, laughing at me.

I mimed wiping it away as I grinned, an idea coming to mind. Lifting my taco dress over my head. I stepped in front of the TV in nothing else. It was laundry day, after all, and I'd put everything through the wash already.

The guys stopped the smirks, and the teasing glints dropped away as they took in my naked flesh. It always felt nice when your men adored your body exactly as it was.

Their tight shorts began to grow tighter as particular members in the front started to harden. I sauntered forward, my eyes on all three of them spread out on the sofa.

"What were you saying about drool? Hmm?"

In typical Slade fashion, as soon as I was close, he pulled me to him. His hands were hot against my flesh as he massaged my butt, placing me over his lap. My legs straddled him, my hands running up his beautifully inked chest as I stared into his eyes.

The need to tease him rose in me, and I turned, pulling Zane to me, kissing him as I moved my hand to free his cock. Slade growled beneath me, but it only made me hotter.

Wrapping my fingers around Zane, his head fell back as I began to pump his thick dick in my hand, squeezing it at the base as I twisted it up. Glancing over at Simon, I winked as I moved and put my butt closer to him. He took the opportunity for it was, and as I placed my lips around Zane, Simon plunged his fingers into my pussy.

I moaned around Zane, my eyes rolling to the back of my head as I fell into a rhythm. I could hear Slade growling more as this occurred over him and not to him, but it honestly only made it sexier for me. When he realized I wouldn't stop, he gave up on the pouting and began to play with my breasts, pinching my nipples in retaliation.

Simon's tongue landed on my center, and I

opened my mouth more to moan, taking Zane even deeper. It became difficult to follow the sensations as he licked and sucked my clit, pumping his fingers in and out. I had a feeling he was trying to get me to squirt, since the twins didn't believe he'd done it.

My eyes began to water as I sucked Zane, and I knew I was hitting my limit of sensations as my legs began to tremble. When Slade bit down on my nipple, giving me the slightest bit of pain, I erupted, blacking out as I came hard.

"Holy shit," someone said as I panted, my body trembling in aftershocks. I barely remembered to swallow as Zane came down my throat with his own grunt.

As soon as he stilled, I was lifted and speared on Slade's dick. He'd waited long enough and was taking what he wanted now. I fell forward onto his chest, and he gently pushed my hair back as he peppered soft and sweet kisses over my face. I knew he was giving me time to adjust to him and to come down from my high, and I appreciated it.

"Watching you squirt all over Simon was one of the sexiest things I've ever seen, Peach. Now, ride me so I can watch you bounce on my dick."

Smiling, I lifted up with his help and began to bounce on him like he wanted, my moans building as the pleasure from the angle took hold. I looked over and found Zane watching, his flaccid dick lying against this stomach. Glancing to the other side, I found Simon stroking his, so I beckoned him to come closer. With a grin, he stood and bent down to kiss me.

"Remember that one time when you both were in the same hole?" I whispered, holding his face. Simon grinned wider, licking his lips at the thought. He moved closer, placing his knees close to mine on the couch.

"What are you doing?" Slade asked, stopping his thrusts.

"Think you can handle two?" I asked, twisting my head to look at him. The heat in his eyes said he was down for it.

"I should lay down; it will be easier," Slade said, moving to take Simon's vacated spot and lying at an angle. Staying upright, I helped Simon move into position again as he began to push his cock in alongside Slade's. The fullness was more than I remembered, and I moaned as my legs started to tense and shake again.

Simon pushed in a little more, stopping to take a few deep breaths as we adjusted. When he was finally in, I felt so full I thought I would burst.

"There's no way you can move. I'll break," I wheezed, the fullness getting to me.

"Lay back. We got you, Peach."

Following his command, I laid on his chest, my back to his front, as they began to work together, moving in and out in tandem. It didn't take long for me to crest again, especially when Zane moved to the side of the couch and found my clit and boobs to give attention to.

"You're so beautiful like this, Lenn," Simon sighed, straining as he tried to keep his orgasm at bay.

I couldn't speak, the pleasure too much, so I nodded, urging them on. They both moved a few more times before I felt them unloading, grunting their releases, and sending me over the edge.

We laid there for a few minutes, panting as we caught our breath, and all I could do was smile.

"I love you guys."

"I love you's," were chorused back, making me feel even fuller than having two cocks in my vagina simultaneously.

Now, that was a tongue twister.

I knew life wasn't guaranteed to always go my way or even be perfect from here on out. But I didn't need it to be. Because going through the messy bits was worth it if I got to do them with these three.

We'd left on this journey to honor a friend, a

fellow rebel, and in the end, we'd all found the part of ourselves we'd been missing.

Slade reconnected with his dad, healing a past wound he hadn't realized was still open.

Simon found a new passion to develop, showing himself he wasn't one-dimensional.

Zane discovered a new path to explore, learning that he could like other things and it not take away from being a vet.

And I found that anything was possible on the open road as long as you had a little faith in yourself.

Epilogue

DARCIE

MY HEADLIGHTS BOUNCED as I turned down the dark road. I had no clue where I was, but I was grateful I had a piece of mail with Lennox's address, or I would've been screwed. When I set off toward her house, I hadn't been thinking about the logistics of it, knowing I just needed to get away from Chase. Away from the scene.

Now, as I took my last turn down her road, I worried I was overstepping. She seemed so happy when I talked to her last week. I didn't want to ruin that. I also hoped I had the timing right, and that she was back by now. If not, maybe I could sleep in the barn or something until morning and figure out a different plan.

Settled, I slowed as I approached the driveway, the lights on giving me a sense of hope and dread.

Shit, I was a lousy friend dragging her into this mess, but I hoped that I wouldn't have to be alone in it.

Thoughts of everything swirled in my head, and I knew I couldn't sit out here all night. I was here. I needed to see this through.

Grabbing my bag, I climbed out of the car and headed toward the front door. A motion-sensor light flared to life, causing me to jump back in alarm, my heart racing.

Taking a few steps up to the porch, I sucked in a breath as I stared at the door. My hands were stained red, and my clothes were covered in odd spots from Chase's blood. Shit. I couldn't do this. I couldn't be that friend who showed up and brought terrible news when she was getting everything she wanted.

Turning to go, I vowed to find another solution after getting some sleep. I only took one step when the door squeaked open behind me.

"Darcie?" her voice called out. "Darcie! It is you. What are you doing here? Where are you going?" Lennox's voice instantly soothed something in me, and despite knowing I was awful for bringing her into this, the comfort of her won out in the end.

Spinning around, I couldn't stop the tears as they began to fall down my cheeks. Lennox's smile dropped as she took me in, bloodstains and all.

"Darce, what happened? Are you hurt? Guys,

come help!" she yelled back into the house, followed by accompanying footsteps.

Before I could get any words out, I was ushered into her house as she began to immediately fawn over me, looking for a sign of injury. I couldn't help it, the tears fell in earnest, and I realized how much I'd missed my friend, how much I'd missed having someone in my corner.

"Ssh, it's alright. Whatever it is, we'll fix it. Just talk to me, Darce," she said, rocking me in her arms. I loved that she didn't even care if she got blood on her. That was the type of friend Lennox was.

"It's not mine," I managed to say as someone hurried in with a bowl of water and a rag. "I'm okay, but I need your help."

The End… well, sort of.
Find out what happens next in *Beautiful Envy*, and catch Lennox and the guys in *Verging* as they go on tour with the band.

Afterword

I hope you enjoyed Lennox's Open Road adventure. It was fun to dive back into the Tattooed Hearts world. Lennox always makes me laugh, and Slade just smolders. While this is the end of their story, they will make appearances in Friendship & Lyrics, Penny's and Poppy's stories.

If you read Beautiful Agony, then you know why Darcie shows up at the end. Her story will be next. I couldn't help but have her end this story, so hopefully, you don't hate me too much for that slight cliffy.

I want to thank Emma and Megan for pushing me through this book. I can never say enough thanks to you both. I also want to thank Lindsay for reading through my words no matter what.

Thank you to Esther for lending me her name.

She won a prize in my reader group to be put into a book. I hope this Esther who love Lennox was a good representation of you.

If you loved this book, consider leaving a review. It helps authors more than you could know. Thanks to all of my readers. You guys are why I push through the blocks and keep publishing.

As always, thanks to my husband for supporting and encouraging me. I love you, babe.

Also by Kris Butler

For the most up to date look at my releases. Check out all my books here: https://authorkrisbutler.com/my-books

The Council Series

(Completed series)

Damaged Dreams

Shattered Secrets

Fractured Futures

Bosh Bells & Epic Fails

The Council Series: The complete omnibus

The Order Duet (Council Spinoff)

Stiletto Sins

Lipstick Lies

Dark Confessions

(Completed series)

Dangerous Truths

Dangerous Lies

Dangerous Vows

Reckless (Cami's Novella)

Relentless (Nat's Novella)

Dangerous Love

Tattooed Hearts Duet

Tattooed Hearts Completed Duet

Riddled Deceit (Part 1)

Smudged Lines (Part 2)

Open Road

Music City Diaries

Beautiful Agony

Beautiful Envy

Friendship & Lyrics

Vibing: A Vacation Rom-Com

Sinners Fairytales

(standalone)

Pride

About the Author

Kris Butler writes under a pen name to have some separation from her everyday life. Never expecting to write a book, she was surprised when an author friend encouraged her to give it a try and how much she enjoyed it. Having an extensive background in mental health, Kris hopes to normalize mental health issues and the importance of talking about them with her characters and books. Kris is a southern girl at heart but lives with her husband and adorable furbaby somewhere in the Midwest. Kris is an avid fan of Reverse Harem and hopes to add a quirky and new perspective to the emerging genre. If you enjoyed her book, please consider leaving a review. You can contact her the following ways and follow Kris's journey as a new author on social media.